A Murder of Crows

Evelyn Flood

Evelyn

A Murder of Crows
Evelyn Flood

First published by Evelyn Flood in 2024

ISBN: 9798884095106
Imprint: Independently published

Copyright 2024 by Evelyn Flood

All rights reserved. This book or any portion thereof may not be reproduced or used in any manner whatsoever without the express written permission of the publisher, except for the use of brief quotations in a book review.

Cover by Jodie-Leigh Plowman at JODIELOCKS DESIGNS

Content Overview

This book contains references to gang war, violence, knife crime, gun crime, sexual assault (non-penetrative), suicide, murder, drugs, trafficking and rape (off page).

IN LOVING DEDICATION

For Nick.
Because I could never write a book with Italian characters, and not dedicate it to you.
I wish you were here to see it, even though I'd never let you read it.

Contents

1. Caterina — 1
2. Caterina — 3
3. Dante — 16
4. Caterina — 19
5. Caterina — 26
6. Domenico — 30
7. Caterina — 36
8. Caterina — 47
9. Caterina — 54
10. Dante — 60
11. Giovanni — 69
12. Caterina — 73
13. Caterina — 77
14. Caterina — 83

15.	Domenico	91
16.	Caterina	96
17.	Caterina	102
18.	Caterina	105
19.	Caterina	112
20.	Caterina	115
21.	Domenico	120
22.	Caterina	125
23.	Caterina	130
24.	Dante	139
25.	Caterina	142
26.	Caterina	147
27.	Caterina	157
28.	Caterina	166
29.	Luciano	169
30.	Caterina	171
31.	Caterina	175
32.	Caterina	181
33.	Caterina	188
34.	Dante	191
35.	Caterina	194
36.	Caterina	200
37.	Luciano	203
38.	Caterina	206

39.	Caterina	210
40.	Caterina	213
41.	Luciano	216
42.	Caterina	219
43.	Luciano	224
44.	Luciano	228
45.	Caterina	231
46.	Caterina	241
47.	Dante	252
A Murder of Crows playlist		254
Stalk me		256

CATERINA

"*My carissimo.*"

Despite myself, my lips twist up in a wry smile as my father's voice echoes through the phone. Pressing it to my ear, I glance around as I make my way through the campus.

"Papa. How is everyone?"

He coughs down the phone, the phlegm from his throat clogging up his voice as he speaks. "Bunch of assholes, always wanting more. Matteo è proprio un cagacazzo."

I bite the inside of my cheek. My cousin Matteo is indeed a fucking asshole. "What did he do now?"

"Nothing you need to concern yourself with." Papa sighs. "The Fuscos have been getting into things they shouldn't. I had to get involved. Watch your back."

Pausing at the edge of the cream-colored building, I frown. "Anything I need to be aware of?"

He clicks his tongue. "I want you to concentrate on why you're there, carissimo. Plenty of time for the rest when you're home."

"Papa," I fight to keep my voice even. "You know it doesn't work like that. How am I supposed to run things here if you're keeping information from me? The Fusco heir is *here*. It puts me at a disadvantage."

"Bah." I can hear him waving his damn hand, the same way he does every time he decides there's something that I don't need to know. I catch myself grinding my teeth and clamp my lips together. "That's life, Caterina. You don't always have all the answers. You work with what you have. In my day, we didn't have any of these politics."

My eyes squeeze shut, my grip on the phone tightening.

"Caterina," his voice is chastising. "This is your role."

My jaw clenches as the call cuts off.

Well, that's fucking irritating.

My mood doesn't improve as I storm across the campus. I purposely stalk straight down the border line, maintaining eye contact with a couple of Morellis on the other side until they look down.

A dangerous game, but an amusing one.

Pausing before the red-brick building, I take a deep breath.

I need a clear head. My father might be the *capo dei capi*, the leader and head of the American mafia, but here, all eyes are on me. His one and only female heir.

Assessing. Judging.

Catching my reflection in the mirrored glass of the front doors, I cast a quick eye over my appearance, making sure there's nothing out of place. My hands don't move to flatten my hair. I don't lean forward to confirm the wings of my eyeliner are perfect.

Caterina Corvo is *always* perfect.

In public, at least.

Caterina

A gang of crows is called a murder.

And as my scarlet heels jab down into the soaked carpet, the moniker has never felt so appropriate.

"The crows are circling," I murmur, and the circle in front of me parts. Dom turns. He scans me, his mouth tightening, but he doesn't mention my lateness as I step up beside him, my eyes on the body responsible for the dark red liquid beneath my feet.

It twists, and my mouth curls up as I glance at Dom. "You left something for me? How kind."

The man – and he is a man in our world, despite the slight puffiness in his cheeks that signify the last vestiges of his teen years – opens his eyes with a wheeze, flickering them around until they land on me, widening with recognition.

His choke sends a large clot of blood flying from his mouth, and I glance down with mild disinterest as it spatters next to my shoes.

I crouch, balancing my elbows on my thighs as I scan him. "Hello, Anton."

His wheezing breaths fill the air, but he doesn't ask why I'm here, doesn't beg for mercy.

Something that feels a little like respect fills my chest, but it's choked down underneath the revulsion. "We seem to have a situation."

Straightening back up, I stand still as the group around me begins to circle Anton. Silent as they move, it jolts him into trying to sit up.

"Please," he starts to blubber. "I didn't know!"

"Tut, tut." My lips twitch up into a smile. "The time for lies is over, Anton. You wove your little stories so prettily, but we're at the end now."

When he grabs for my foot, I slam my heel down, directly into his wrist. The punch of the bladed tips through his skin sends screaming echoing through the soundproofed building.

"Loyalty," I say softly, as the screams peel off into choked sobs. "Loyalty is everything, Anton. It's the backbone of who we are. And you broke your vow. You swore Omerta, but at the first test, you betrayed our entire way of life. You shared information with outsiders that did not belong to you."

Turning, I wait for the moving crowd to stop.

"I sentence you to die." My voice rings out, echoing off the walls in the silence. "For breaking Omerta. May your soul be judged in hell, as it has been here."

Anton begins to weep, red-tinted tears tracking down his face, but he stays silent as I reach down and drag the thin stiletto from the back of my heel.

"Is there anything you wish to say, before I carry out your sentence?" My words make him jolt, his eyes flicking from side to side before they settle on the blade in my hand.

"A gun," he whispers, his eyes moving to mine. "Please. Not this way."

My hands don't shake as I reach out, pressing the blade against his lip, the tip disappearing into his mouth. He closes his eyes, his shoulders slumping.

"Traitors don't get to choose their path to hell." My voice is cold. "Goodbye, Anton."

The blade is silent as it thrusts into his mouth, his body parting like butter beneath the sharp steel before he collapses into himself, sliding off my blade and hitting the floor with a dull thump.

Carefully, I wipe the blade down with the cloth Dom hands me. My Crows wait in silence, wait for me to finish my cleaning and slide the stiletto back into my heel before I speak.

"The Courtyard. Three days."

Two junior soldiers step forward when Dom nods at them. Grabbing Anton under his arms, they begin to drag him from the room as the rest follow, a silent vigil.

Only Dom stays, his eyes lingering on me until I finally look at him. "What?"

"Three days is a long time. His brother is here."

Fuck.

I forgot his brother joined us recently. I swallow back the tinge of regret, pushing past Dom. "You're my enforcer, not my conscience, Dom. Three days. We don't fuck around with traitors."

I need air. He follows me, his irritation a familiar prickle against my skin. "Cat."

I stop, turning and wiping every inch of expression from my face. "Do not challenge me," I say in a low voice. "Remember your place, Domenico."

His face tightens, and fuck if I don't hate myself a little. But he steps back, his own expression fading as he nods his head. "As you wish. I'll be in the Courtyard."

He doesn't wait for me to respond before he twists, moving away from me with his shoulders up and his head raised high.

He'll do as I ask. But I still feel like shit as I head back the way I came. Blood spatters my arms, and the few students I come across give me a wide, respectful berth. People are silent as they watch, their eyes pricking my skin until I reach my apartment.

My key jangles in the lock, a hot shower and a strong coffee screaming my name. No time for that, though. I need to clean up and get back out there, pristine and polished as though I haven't just gutted a man.

My thoughts are tangled up in the betraying piece of shit now displayed out in the Courtyard like an art sculpture and Dom's face as he walked away from me, and I don't notice the shadow in a place where it shouldn't be before it's too late.

I throw my shoulder against the door, and a male grunt sounds. The door is shoved back, and I stagger, my hand dropping for my dagger as I whip it out and throw myself at my *very fucking unwelcome* visitor.

"Who the fuck said that you could come here?" I snarl, pressing the blade into his neck.

A pair of vivid green eyes meet mine, and I gasp as he shoves me back, grabbing my wrists and flipping us. My stiletto blade hangs uselessly at my side as Dante presses himself into me, green eyes scanning my face.

"Caterina," he murmurs. The door behind me clicks shut as he pushes me into the wood. "Heard you had a bad day. I've missed you."

Sighing, I allow my body to relax under his, just enough for the smirk to curl the edges of his mouth before I slam my head forward and into his nose. He staggers away from me with a curse. "Fucking hell, Cat!"

Smirking, I flip my blade in my hand. "You think you can come into my territory, enter my *home*, without an invite?"

Dante gives me a side eye, wincing as he feels his nose. "Damn. Might be broken."

"Whoops." I smile. Dante's hand falls from his face, and he crosses his arms.

We weigh each other up, both of us breathing heavily. Anton's blood feels heavy on my skin, and Dante flicks his eyes over my arms. "I appear to be missing an informant. Thought you might need a little help."

I raise an eyebrow. "From you? I don't think so. My man is dead because of you."

And his little contacts in the feds. Anton had too many fingers in too many pies, and not enough brains to keep track of them all. Thankfully, we caught him before he had the chance to do any damage by mouthing off to the cops.

He waves his hand. How easily he dismisses the loss of one of mine. He wouldn't be so blasé if the shoe were on the other foot. "You hated Anton. He was an asshole. Excuse me if I'm not sobbing over his corpse."

My lips press together, refusing to acknowledge the truth in his words. "How did you get in?"

He tilts his head to the side, his smile slow and curling. "Thought I'd test your security. Seems you have a few holes, *principessa*."

I fight to keep my irritation off my face, the reminder that nowhere is truly safe here no matter what boundaries we pretend to put in place. "Get out."

He steps forward instead. "I can take that edge off for you," he murmurs. "That fizzing in your veins. The shaking in your hands. It's been too long, Cat."

My palms curl into fists. "Once was enough. It wasn't particularly impressive."

His face drops, the barb hitting home. Nothing quite insults a male like throwing shade at their sexual prowess. "You didn't say that when you were crying out my name."

My face flushes in response, and he moves closer, noticing my hesitation. I stiffen when his hand reaches out, but his hand wraps around my braid, tugging my head back as he moves into me, pressing his face into my neck.

"Are you wet for me now?" he whispers into my skin. "If I slide my hand into that sweet pussy of yours, would you soak my fingers?"

My eyes slide closed. A single moment to enjoy the heat curling in my stomach. He actually looks surprised when I shove him back. "I'm not one of your little V'Arezzo whores," I snap back at him. "We had one quick fuck months ago, Dante. That's it."

He snarls at me. "We're both fucking adults, Cat. It was damn good sex, and we're intelligent enough not to let it get in the fucking way."

There are fifty reasons why this is not a fucking good idea. A hundred reasons why I should throw him out of my room, rip my so-called security team new assholes and banish any thoughts of Dante V'Arezzo from my head.

But I'm *tired*.

So, I step back until my back is pressed against the door, letting a taunting smile play over my lips. Dante runs a hand over his face, his gaze focused as I drop my hands to the buttons on my leather trousers.

I flick one open, then another.

"What are you doing, Caterina?"

My grin feels savage as I push the trousers down, kicking them off over my heels. "You seem to be in a giving mood, V'Arezzo."

I dip my fingers underneath the edge of my lace underwear, and Dante groans under his breath as he watches my fingers move over my pussy. I pinch my clit, pushing my hips out towards him.

"Get on your knees," I murmur, "and you can have a taste."

I expect him to balk. Heirs don't kneel for anyone, and certainly not another heir. But he steps forward until the hard outline of his dick is pressed against my stomach. His whisper feels hot against my ear.

"There are more ways to submit than on your knees, Caterina Corvo."

I draw in a breath as he drops to his knees at my feet. Large fingers curl into the edges of my underwear, yanking them until they rip. My head bangs back into the door, and my hands move to his shoulders as he curls his hands around my thighs and lifts me onto his face.

"F-fuck."

I hope he can't hear my strangled gasp, his face buried between my legs as he seals his lips around my clit and sucks. The edges of his stubble drag across my skin, and my heels dig into his back as he holds me in place, fucking me with his tongue, sliding in and out until I'm a panting, shaking mess on the edge of what promises to be fucking *fireworks*.

He pulls his head back, looking up at me with a smirk. His lower face is soaked with me as his hands squeeze my skin. "Say my name, principessa, and I'll let that little cunt of yours come."

Mother*fucker*.

My hands move to his head, and I tug the hair at the back of his neck roughly. "Just get the fucking job done, V'Arezzo. Stop trying to make this a fucking thing."

In response, he turns and sinks his fucking teeth into the sensitive skin of my inner thigh. "Say it," he demands. When I shake my head, he traces his tongue softly up my slit, enough that the building beckoning of my impending orgasm starts to douse.

"You're an asshole," I grit out, and his low laugh vibrates through me. He drops my legs to the floor abruptly, making me stagger.

Dante gets to his feet, his hands moving to his jeans. "Come here, Caterina."

"*Testa di cazzo*," I hiss back at him, and he tsks, clicking his tongue.

"That wasn't very nice. Don't you want to come?"

I'm fucking dripping, sagging against the door as he pulls his cock out, tattooed hands stroking it up and down. I was *so* fucking close.

"I hate you," I throw at him, and he grins. "I know. That's what makes this so fucking good."

I don't fight as he hoists me again, notching the head of his cock against my entrance and thrusting inside. My forehead presses against his shoulder as he fucks me roughly, the sound of our bodies slapping together in the air and my door thudding behind us. Dante's movements pick up, and he presses his lips to my shoulder, making me twist away.

"Just sex," I gasp, and I'm rewarded with a particularly hard thrust.

"*Fottuta tentazione*," he snarls, and I cry out as teeth sink into my neck, the sharp bite of pain yanking my climax from me with force as I shake, Dante's arms holding me upright as I hold onto him. His release follows moments after, his groan guttural in my ear as I feel the wet heat of him between my legs.

I give myself a few seconds to catch my breath. A few, short seconds of pretending that this is anything else than an itch to be scratched before I shove at his shoulders. "Put me down."

"Give a man a minute at least," he mutters. His hands loosen, my feet dropping down to the floor as I disentangle myself, trying to drag back together the pieces that make up Caterina Corvo. The pieces that Dante has to see. I'm careful to wipe any expression from my face, any possible giveaway before I turn to him.

"You know where the door is. Apparently." I duck under his arm, ignoring his muttered curse as I head towards the bathroom. "Don't come here again, V'Arezzo."

I slam the door behind me, pressing my back against it as I take a deep breath and listen. There's a rustling, the sound of Dante pulling his jeans up. And a pause.

"Pretend all you want, *tentazione*," he calls, and I close my eyes. "But your body can't lie to me."

I bite back the argument on my tongue, shove down the urge to storm back out and shout at him again until we're tangled up in bedding, our bodies locked together in savage, fluid movement. Until I can forget the smell of blood in my nose, the feel of my blade embedded in flesh.

The feeling of taking a life. Another tick for the devil's tally.

But that's a fool's dream. My front door slams shut, and thirty seconds later, I'm buried under hot water, scrubbing away any lingering traces of Anton and of the man who just spent an hour buried between my thighs.

Washing away my sins. It's hard to know which is worse.

For one, I'm answerable to whatever deity is up there. Or down there, depending on how you look at these things.

For the other, I'm answerable to my family.

I know which I'd prefer. It takes longer than I'd like to admit to put myself back together, my hair braided tightly against my face. I collect a new pair of black shiny stilettos from my wardrobe, slowly sliding my daggers into them.

I then spend a good fifteen minutes swearing at and then trying to cover the fucking bite mark on my neck.

I'm still cursing under my breath when I reach the Courtyard.

The crowd has already gathered, silent and still as I weave between them. A path miraculously opens up, and I pause at the edges.

The Crows are circling.

V'Arezzo. Morelli. Asante. Fusco. More are filtering in behind me, their footsteps echoing in the harsh silence as the crowd watches the Crows demonstrate exactly what we do to traitors.

Anton's eyes are still open, the white lined with cracks of red as he lays on the ground at the base of the northern red oak tree that stands in the middle of our campus. Blood continues to pool beneath his head, a cushion against the stone slabs.

Maybe elsewhere, at another college or university, students might be whispering. Shocked, crying, asking why the fuck there's a body displayed in public.

But not here.

Here, the watchers are pale and silent. Understanding the warning we're kindly giving them; in the only neutral place we have.

There are no second chances.

A dirty blonde head of hair catches my eye. Paul Maranzano marches with the Crows, his eyes dull as he looks away from his brother's body. Dom is behind him, his eyes focused on the back of Paul's head.

He doesn't look at me.

Crossing my arms, I watch, blanketed in the isolation of being a predator amongst prey. The crowd gives me a wide berth.

At least, most of them do.

A low whistle sounds at my side, the low voice warmer than it should be given the circumstances. "You Crows really do know how to make an impression."

I don't look at him. "Morelli."

"Caterina." He shifts, crossing his arms to mirror mine. Dom is looking over now, the faintest edges of a frown pulling at his mouth, but he doesn't move from his spot.

"Tell me," Luc presses. "Do you eat them afterwards? Scavenge them?"

I turn to him then. Even I can appreciate that Luciano Morelli, heir to the Morelli crime family, is a beautiful man. He was a pretty boy, angelic even, but as a man, his wings have grown darker. His eyes almost twinkle as he meets my gaze, deep hazel eyes set against olive skin. Even the messy hawk on top of his head looks carelessly perfect, the sides carefully shaved into strong lines. The slight crook in his nose only adds to his charm.

And he fucking knows it.

"Who knows," I say softly. "Maybe you'll find out one of these days, Luciano."

His jaw tightens at my not-so-subtle admonishment. Giving me a short nod, he melts back into the crowd. I scan the people around us, catching Dante leaning against a wall in the corner. His enforcer, Rocco, stands beside him, but Dante's eyes aren't on the Crows.

No. They're on me, and my neck.

My hand twitches with the urge to reach up and cover the mark he made, the brand he tried to place on my skin. My make-up has enough coverage to blot it out completely. No-one will be able to see it.

My fingers flex at my side as I step forward. My Crows stop immediately, but it's Paul I move to. His eyes are on the ground, his jaw tight and hands clenched. He flinches when I put my hand on his shoulder.

"I'm sorry for your loss," I murmur, and he shudders. His eyes are wet when he looks up at me.

"I didn't know—,"

I cut off his panicked explanations. "I know, Paul. Start the call."

Comprehension fills his face, along with confusion. "But – but he was a traitor. He broke Omerta."

His voice cracks on the last word. Paul is a new arrival, one of the youngest and newest here as a *cugine* – a junior soldier, nowhere near made man status. Pity twists my chest. He'll see far more than this before his time here is done. I can't shelter him from it.

But I can give him this.

"Call for your brother, Paul," I whisper. "The Crows will follow."

He nods shakily, this boy who turned into an adult the moment he watched his brother be executed for treason. Blowing out a breath, he takes a few seconds to compose himself before he raises his head.

His cry echoes out into the Courtyard, a mournful wail of grief that hits me directly in the chest, even as I take a breath and follow his lead.

One after another. Our grief rises up, one after another, until the space around us is filled with the cries.

Hear us.

We have not called for anyone in our time here. Dante straightens, his face slacking a little before he wipes the expression from his face. Luciano, for once empty of his charm, stands silently before us, watching.

We are the Crows.

And we mourn the loss of one of our own.

When our voices trail away, our harsh cries silenced by the limitations of our own throats, I turn to Dom. Perhaps he was right, earlier. No need to hammer this particular message home.

The silence in the Courtyard tells me that the message has already been received.

"Burn him," I say hoarsely. "Send the ashes to his parents. I'll speak with them."

Paul stiffens on my other side, but he doesn't argue, doesn't ask for any more. Anton is lucky to have received the call at all, and he knows it. I did it for him, to try and nudge one of mine in the right direction and avoid his heart hardening with resentment and anger.

But my mercy only extends so far. And our traitors do not rest with family.

Dante

Rocco stands silently next to me, watching the show, but my mind isn't on the update that he's just stopped right in the middle of, his attention drawn by the Crows.

No, my mind is well and truly on the infuriating woman in front of me. Caterina tips her head up, her cries easily identifiable amongst the calls from the other Crows.

She grieves despite everything, and the smallest pang of guilt hits my chest. Anton Maranzano is dead because of his double crossing. He wasn't even a particularly useful mole, too full of self-importance to have much room for anything worthwhile in his head.

He made his own choices, trying to claw his way up in a world that was always going to chew him up and spit him out. I'm not about to shed tears over a traitor.

Still, I felt a flip in my chest when the Corvos began to circle. They know how to put on a show, reveling in their crow nickname. Their methods are common knowledge but rarely seen in public. Until now, at least.

Cat meets my eyes, and I dip my chin in acknowledgement.

Message received.

I'm only half-listening to Rocco as he picks up where he left off, but then my head snaps to the side. "Say that again."

His lips press together. "Nicoletta Fusco is dead."

That explains Gio's absence. Normally he'd be here, skulking in corners and snarling at everyone, but he's nowhere to be seen. "How?"

Rocco shifts on his feet. "Not sure yet."

The oldest daughter of the Fusco crime lord is dead. It's unexpected, and I don't like surprises. "Find out."

My lips press together as the Crows melt away, leaving Anton's body where it sits against the northern oak. Red leaves sway on the breeze, a similar color to the rusty puddle underneath.

Cat talks quietly to her second, a hulking tattooed dark haired fucker who looks at her with far too much possession in his gaze. Domenico Rossi is a quiet force in his own right. He'd have to be, since he's led the Crows in Cat's absence for *months*.

Curiosity prickles me. Here one day, gone the next. Unusual for an heir to be away for so long, especially when the five crime families have been so focused on the current intake. This is the first time in the history of the so-called Mafia University that all five heirs have attended at the same time.

Battle lines are being drawn.

Things are shifting between the families of the American mafia, and I can't tell which way the cards are going to fall. Not yet.

But if the daughter of the Fusco don is dead, then there's danger in the air.

Rocco follows my gaze. "Still pining?"

"Fuck off," I snap. Nobody else is close enough to hear Rocco's low laugh. He's the only one I'd allow to get away with it.

"How is our little female heir?"

His tone is mildly scornful as we fall into step, leaving the Courtyard to make our way to the dining hall. The dons insist that we maintain a routine.

We might be killing each other at four, but at five? You sit your ass down and eat dinner together like *civilized people*.

"Don't underestimate her," I caution under my breath. Cat doesn't look at me as we pass by, her focus entirely on what her second is telling her. "All heirs are dangerous, Rocco."

And the woman burning daggers into my back could well be the most dangerous of all.

CATERINA

"He's staring at you."

Dom sounds on the edge of violence, and I cross my arms to avoid punching him in the face, just like when we were kids. "Fuck all the way off with that shit, Domenico. Anything useful to say?"

Dom tips his head, but his jaw still ticks as he shifts to block me from Dante's view. Just to mess with him, I take a step to the right. His nostrils flare. "Cat."

Relenting, I roll my eyes. "Worried I'll faint away at the feel of his eyes on me? I think we're safe."

Dom drops his eyes to my neck. "You sure about that?"

I take a step closer. "You don't get to lecture me about my choices, Domenico. You want to be my enforcer? Spend less time giving me the fucking puppy eyes and more time on what's important."

His eyes shutter. "Fine. Nicoletta Fusco was found dead. Butchered. It was violent."

His abrupt switch makes my thoughts stumble over each other as they process. "Motherfucker."

My mind instantly moves to Matteo, but I dismiss it. None of us go after women or children.

It's almost sacred. There is only one exception, and it sure as fuck wasn't the shy girl who spent most of her time with her head buried in a book. No, the only exception across the Cosa Nostra, the five crime families of mafia America... is me.

What a lucky bitch.

But my father's words from our call earlier play through my head, and I frown. The coincidence... I can't ignore the possibility, unpalatable as it is.

I didn't know Nicoletta well, heavily protected as she was by her father and brother. But we met a few times over the years at prearranged Cosa Nostra socials, mixers, and she was always sweet.

The last thing I thought I'd ever say about a Fusco. "I didn't see Giovanni here."

Dom shakes his head. "Word is he's about to burn the whole fucking country down. They've put everything they have on it. He left this morning."

I can imagine. Of the five of us that make up the heirs, Gio is easily the most intense. Stefano could probably give him a run for his money, but he never says enough to really cinch the title.

"I don't like this," I say in a low voice, and he nods. "Watching brief."

Dante walks past with Rocco, and we pivot, following them as they make their way to the dining hall. Everyone on campus is heading that way, a stream of bodies that block up the entrance as everyone hustles to get in. I catch a couple of my Crows in a shoving war with a few

Asantes, and one of them pales as they catch my eye, stepping back and hissing at the others.

Dante passes through first, Dom and I following.

"Fucking hate this shit," Dom mutters, and I huff in agreement. Part of the deal brokered by the families' states that all attendees at the university must eat together. They didn't stop there, either.

"I'll get you a plate." Dom walks off before I can respond, leaving me to stare at his retreating back. Dante turns around as Rocco walks off to the section they've claimed for the V'Arezzos. "You coming?"

I brush past him, picking up his low intake of breath. "Are you?"

We both make our way to the head table. Five seats, set up almost like fucking thrones. One for each heir.

We break bread together every night. Breakfast and lunch, we can sit anywhere we want, but at dinner, the heirs dine together.

Luciano is already there, leaning back with a vacant expression that clears as my heels click against the stone steps. He pulls out the chair next to him. "Little crow."

"Morelli." Ignoring the silent invite, I yank out the chair at the end of the table and drop into it. This way, I only have to put up with one of them.

Dante gets pulled back by one of his men, and I breathe a quiet sigh of relief when Stefano pushes past him, pulling out the chair next to me. Dante's eyes flick to us, but he doesn't say anything as he follows, taking the seat next to Stefano that Luc pulled out for me.

"So kind of you to save me a seat, Morelli." His voice is low, but it carries down the table.

"I'm nothing if not accommodating, V'Arezzo," Luc responds smoothly.

Ignoring the testosterone overload, I watch the Fusco table. They sit silently, none of the posturing and good-natured ribbing we'd normally see. Their eyes keep flicking to the empty seat on the other side of Luc.

"Nicoletta Fusco," Stefano murmurs, and I turn to look at him. He's shaved his head again, the short brown hair he used to have disappearing beneath a buzz cut. His tattooed hands tap the table, just once. "You know anything?"

Dom walks up with a plate of food in his hands, his eyes moving between us before I wave at him to come forward. He holds it out. "I tested it."

"Thanks." I take it from him, my stomach grumbling as the scent of rich, freshly-cooked food hits me and he returns back to our group.

Returning my attention to Stefano, I wait until I've taken a bite of my steak to respond, weighing up my options.

None of the heirs are allies. Not really. It's impossible to form true friendship in our world. But the Asantes and the Corvos are probably closer than most. My father meets Salvatore Asante regularly for poker, each of them testing the other. An alliance isn't formal, but there's something.

"Not yet." I keep my voice low. "You?"

He shakes his head. The rest of our meal is silent, my ears pricked to try to catch Luc and Dante's quiet discussion. Stefan stays silent next to me. He probably used up his quota of words for the year with that one question.

Pushing my empty plate away, I glance over at the Crow table. A willowy blonde stares at me beseechingly, practically straining in her chair, and I tilt my head. She's almost bouncing, and when I raise one eyebrow in question, she takes out her phone and waves it exaggeratedly in the air.

Sliding my phone out of my pocket, I angle it away from any curious eyes and flick through my messages. Amie's name is at the top.

Movies and margaritas?

I stare down at the message, considering, before typing a short reply. I watch from the corner of my eye as her phone buzzes in her hand and she does a mini celebratory hand pump, drawing a few eyes her way.

"Making plans?"

I just about hold onto the startled jump of my shoulders at the deep murmur in my ear. Dante's fingers brush the shoulder of my silky bronze blouse, and I roll my eyes. "Did no one ever teach you not to touch what doesn't belong to you, V'Arezzo?"

His lips twitch into a small smile. "Oh, I learned that lesson *very* well."

Asshole. Possessive asshole, which is worse. Ignoring him, I push my seat back, forcing him to take a step back. But only a small one. He invades my space as I get up, the fresh minty scent telling me I'm not the only one who took a shower earlier.

I hope the water was stone fucking cold.

He stares at me, his eyebrows dropping down as I take a very obvious, very long sweeping glance to his smart black shoes and back up.

"Do not," I murmur softly, "make the mistake of thinking that this is more than what it is, V'Arezzo. You're a convenience, and you're pretty, but if you pull any of that bullshit with me, I can find someone else."

He bares his teeth. "Why throw away a good thing? Two heirs, together. Think of the power, Cat."

My head tilts as I glance down the table. Luciano is watching us, his wine glass tilted as he lounges back in his chair.

"Perhaps I am." The words slip out, aiming to wound, to push him away. "But you're not the only pretty heir at this table."

The barb lands. Dante's eyes narrow, and he steps even further into me. "Don't push me on this, Cat."

Scoffing, I shove past him. "Little boys and their toys. You're all the fucking same."

He doesn't follow me, but a hand reaches out, curling around my wrist as I pass Luciano. "For what it's worth, I offer myself for your pleasure anytime, little crow."

I curve my hand around his own wrist, yanking it back until he snarls. My smile is sweet as fucking cotton candy. "Pleasure comes in many forms, Morelli. For me, at least. But maybe not for you."

He doesn't pull away from my grip, leaning into it instead until I'm forced to decide between releasing him and breaking the bone. He spots the hesitation and grins.

"Like you'd want to permanently damage this face."

"Don't tempt me," I mutter. Dropping his wrist, I stalk from the head table, passing the Crows on my way out. Dom half-rises from his seat, but I shake my head.

I'm done for the day. Done with politics, and men who think they know everything.

As I walk past the Fusco table, the tension is bleeding into the air. Pausing, I scan until I reach Leo, Giovanni's enforcer and leader of the Fusco group in Gio's absence. His eyes are vacant, but he turns when someone taps his arm to get his attention as I move up to them.

"I'm sorry about Nicoletta," I say to him directly.

He was close to the Fusco sisters. Closer still to Nicoletta, if the rumors were right. And it seems like they were, because his empty face twists into a snarl, grief and anger leaking in. "I don't want your sympathy, *crow*."

The vehement words take me aback, the tone of his voice bitter. Resentful. And the faces around him are the same, all focused on me with what feels like full-on hatred.

This... this is more than rivalry. Much more than the tenuous push-and-pull, the balance I normally see from them.

"Nevertheless," I say quietly but firmly. My eyes scan the table. Several faces drop, but more still meet my look with their own eyes burning. "You have it."

The whispers start back up, sweeping the dining hall as I spin, not waiting for a response before I leave. But the anger on his face stays with me as I head back to my apartment under the darkening sky, making sure to check the locks several times before pulling out my phone.

I need to speak to my father, but the voicemail kicks in, again. The generic message ends with a beep, and I take a breath.

"Papa, I need to speak with you urgently. Call me back."

I need you to tell me we weren't involved in the murder of Nicoletta Fusco.

Because if the suspicion twisting my stomach is correct, then everything changes. Rules have been broken. The Fuscos will demand vengeance. And I'm here, playing the game blindfolded with one hand tied behind my fucking back.

CATERINA

My heels press into the cream carpet again, leaving little grooves in their wake. The floor is littered with them, hundreds of little pieces of evidence of my own unease as I pace up and down. My phone is dark in my hand. No response.

The unspoken message is clear. My father isn't going to give me anything more than the carefully veiled words he said to me earlier. For now, at least.

I only stop when the knock comes from the door. The familiar *rat-a tat-tat* jogs my memory, and I glance through the peephole before pulling it open.

Amie holds up the jug. "Homemade!"

When I blink at her, she lowers it and grimaces. "You *already* forgot? We organized this literally two hours ago."

When I sigh and stand back, she dances past me, pacing the jug down with a flourish on my polished glass coffee table. "Sorry. It's been a day."

Her shoulders slump, and I immediately feel guilty. As the only genuine friend I've managed to make over the last twenty years, thanks to my father's politics, I should really make more of an effort for Amie. She's the only small slice of normality I get.

Kicking off my heels, I let my feet sink into the carpet as she heads into my kitchenette, digging around in cupboards.

"There's barely any food in here," she calls out. "And *why* do you keep a gun in your cereal cupboard?"

I shrug as she wanders back in with two glasses in her hands. "Easy to reach."

She gives me the side-eye but doesn't comment as she digs around in the little bag she's brought. She pulls out two bottles of wine, three limes and a saltshaker, and I have to laugh. "See? You already knew I wouldn't have that."

"I like to be prepared." She starts setting things up as I duck into the bedroom, shucking off my clothes and replacing them with leggings and a hooded sweatshirt. I take a few minutes to tug out my tight ponytail, massaging my aching skull as I head back to the living room.

Amie bows with a flourish, before she holds out my drink and I take it gratefully. "I needed this."

"I know." She lifts her own glass. "To being a badass Corvo heir."

Scoffing, I clink my glass with hers anyway, taking a few deep gulps that make Amie's eyes fly up into her hairline. "Woah. Rough day? I know you can hold it, but still."

We settle back into the couch, and I rest my aching head against the cool, soft brown leather. "You already know. You called for him too."

"I did." Her voice is more subdued now. "Was it bad? With Anton?"

Sighing, I study the inside of my glass. "It was... it was what he made it. The only person responsible is him. Just another day."

Another day, another death to add to the load weighing down my soul.

"I don't know how you do it. I couldn't."

"We do what we must." Amie isn't part of the soldier hierarchy. She'll never know what it feels like to scrub someone's life-blood from under your nails, to see the swirls of red draining away from your skin as you try to wash the sin away. "It's not something you need to think about, anyway."

When she doesn't respond, I tilt my head, looking towards her. Her blonde hair hides her face as she stares into her own drink. "What is it?"

She clears her throat, cheeks pinking as her shoulders lift in a half-shrug. "Nothing, really. It's just... they brought Francesca Asante in. New tutor for some of us."

Frowning, I try to think. Our tutors work in short sprints, representatives called in from each of the five families on a rotating basis to teach us various topics before being replaced. A fair system, to avoid too much favoritism. And at the end of each day, they leave, the gates closing behind them.

Here, we govern ourselves. Our people answer only to us, the five heirs. And we are answerable only to the dons of the five families. A microcosm of the world that waits for us outside these walls.

"I don't think I know her. What's the class?"

Amie laughs, but there's no humor in her voice. "*Marriage lessons.*"

My margarita lodges in my throat, making me choke. Amie reaches over to thump my back as I splutter. "They what?"

"Apparently, we need to prepare ourselves to be good little wives for our mafia husbands." Amie's words are dry, even as she downs the rest of her drink. "That was always the plan, wasn't it? Soldier or wife.

Either way, everyone here has a role to play. And apparently, this is mine."

"Fucking hell," I mutter in horror. I couldn't think of anything worse. Grabbing my phone, I flick through my emails, looking for any changes to my schedule. "I don't have her."

"Well, you wouldn't," Amie points out. "You're an heir."

And thank fuck for that. The idea of some old biddy coming in and telling me all the ways I need to please my future husband is enough to make my bits shrivel up. "But... has anyone mentioned marriage to you? Your father?"

Amie's dad is my father's enforcer. Aldo is a mountain of a man, silent and scarred, but I can't see him forcing Amie into anything.

"It's been mentioned, but only in terms of future plans." She half-smiles. "I know my path, Cat. I just hope they pick someone decent."

If I were the *capo dei capi*, ruler of all five families like my father, I'd change that shit in a heartbeat. But my hands are tied. As an heir, I only have limited power until I take over.

I open my mouth to promise that I'll speak to my father, but the words get stuck in my throat. He's not even talking to me. And I won't make promises I can't keep.

She sees my face. "I know, Cat. I get it. It's okay."

It's not okay, and we both know it. But Amie holds up her glass, and after a moment, I follow her lead.

"To drinking until we can't feel our faces," she announces.

I shouldn't. I should stay alert. Ready.

But it's been a fucking *day*. So I clink my glass with hers.

"I'll drink to that."

Domenico

Climbing the steps to Cat's living quarters, I'm stopped by two men melting out of the darkness. My hand drops, but then Nicolo's face appears in the dim light, and I relax, pushing the gun back into the holster underneath my jacket. "Boys."

And boys they both are, even if Nicolo is a senior soldier now. I appointed him myself, and oversaw his training. He's working out well so far.

And he proves it, stepping into my path as I go to move past him and Drew. "Sorry, Dom. She doesn't want to be interrupted."

Well, now.

"Careful now, soldier." My words are quiet. "Remember who you're talking to."

Drew blanches, but Nicolo stands his ground. "I'm sorry. But she gave me the order herself."

And Caterina outranks me. My head turns towards her door. "Why?"

I get my answer a moment later. The low thrum of bass echoes out, the pulse of music accompanied by two silhouettes in the window.

My entire body locks up. "Who."

It's not a question. It's a fucking demand. Drew and Nicolo exchange glances, and my blood heats up. I will put them on their fucking backs and fuck the hierarchy.

If she's up there with *him*—

Luckily, Drew blurts out the answer. "Amie."

My whole body relaxes at that, and it's enough to tell me that I'm really in fucking trouble. Shoving the thoughts away, I purse my lips. "Call her."

When Nicolo hesitates, I yank my phone out myself with a curse, hitting her number.

The two men shift on their feet as the phone rings.

And rings.

For fucks' sake.

Ending the call as it goes to her voicemail, I level them both with a look. "I'm her enforcer, *your* senior, and I need to speak with her. Get in my way and I'll put you on night patrol for the next three months. Fridays and Saturdays."

Drew groans, but Nicolo draws himself up. He swallows, but he still meets my eyes. "I'll knock and ask."

I shouldn't want to punish him for doing exactly what I've fucking told him to do. Waving him away with a grunt, I cross my arms and eyeball Drew. He blanches. "How's your training going?"

He grins. "Good, I think. The new routine works better for my knee. Thanks, Dom."

Nodding, I watch as Nicolo knocks hesitantly. Too quiet to be heard over the music, but then he knocks again. Two hard smacks that send the silhouettes in the window flying apart. One moves out of sight, and light spills out as Caterina yanks the door open.

"This had better be fucking good, Nicolo," she snaps. It would be petrifying, if it wasn't for the hiccup at the end.

Rolling my eyes, I push past Drew, taking the last of the steps two at a time. "Take pity on him. I need to talk to you."

She sways a little as she looks at me, and Nicolo seizes the opportunity to slide away, back to his post. Leaving me alone with her.

Caterina's hair, that intoxicating mass of blonde and bronze ringlets, is loose around her face, strands sticking to her forehead damply. Brown eyes, so deep it's difficult to see where her irises end and her pupils begin, watch me closely, still very much assessing despite her inebriation.

Even as I stand there, I can see her putting her building blocks back up, those damn fucking walls of hers sliding into place. For a moment, I despise myself for pulling her away from her evening.

"It won't take long," I say quietly. She purses her lips, but she stands back, letting me in. Amie is sprawled across the couch, very much the worse for wear as she blinks at me blearily. Bottles and glasses are scattered everywhere, and the thumping music dies as Cat flicks it off.

I frown at Amie. "She needs to go home. She's wasted."

"Domenico," she slurs. "Always so commanding."

When I turn back to Cat, there's a look on her face I haven't seen before. She wipes it too quickly for me to identify it, but she sighs as she looks at her friend. "Have Drew and Nic take her."

Like hell am I letting another man past her front door, so I carefully scoop Amie up. She curls her arms around my neck, snuggling her face into my chest as I carry her past Caterina. "Can you get the door?"

Silently, Cat yanks it open as I whistle. After an awkward transfer to Nicolo where Amie hangs onto my neck and Drew has to help peel her fingers off, they set off, and I close the door behind them.

Cat is perched on the end of the couch, her knees drawn up to her chest and her arms wrapped around them. "What is it?"

For a single moment, she looks small. Fragile. Heartbreakingly so. But then she looks up at me with that damn Corvo fire blazing in her eyes, and I realize that I've made a miscalculation.

Because she's *livid*.

"What?" I ask, instead of answering her. "What did I do?"

She looks away from me. "Just tell me why you're here, Dom."

"Not until you tell me why you're pissed off at me."

She almost flies off the couch, advancing towards me. "I'm not pissed off at you."

"Yes, you are," I grit out. She stops a bare inch from my chest, her head just reaching my chin as I look down. "And I need to know why. So get your little tantrum over with and tell me what the *fuck* is the matter with you, so we can get back to business."

She chokes, and I almost smile before her finger jabs into my chest.

"*You*," she snarls. "You turn up to my apartment, ruin my damn evening, make me turn off my music, get all *protective* over *my* best friend and then have the fucking audacity to tell me to *get over myself*?"

I can tell the moment she realizes her mistake. Her mouth snaps shut, cheeks coloring in a way I haven't seen for a long, long time. I haven't seen Cat this loose, this undone, in... too long.

She tries to turn, then, but my hand shoots out, sliding into that perfect bronze mass of curls and cupping the back of her head. My fingers massage her skull as she fights to regain her composure. "You jealous, baby?"

Baby. The endearment slips out, but it feels fucking perfect on my tongue. Nowhere near as perfect as Cat would feel, though. If she'd only fucking admit it, let down those walls for a single damn minute so she can see what's straight in front of her face.

But her face changes, tightening up, the heat fading away. "Don't fuck around with me tonight, Dom," she says quietly. I trace the dark circles beneath her eyes, the exhaustion tightening her face. "Please."

I could push. She knows it, and I know it, and she'd crumble.

For a minute, or maybe even for an hour. A single, blissful hour. And then those walls would be back up, solid as fucking titanium and twice as hard to break down next time.

I need her to see that I'm not just here for a damn good time. I'm in this for the long haul.

But tonight isn't the night. Not when she's drunk, and a little sad, and so fucking tired she's swaying on her feet. So instead, I carefully withdraw my hand, brushing the curls away from her face as she watches me. Instead of yanking her into me, breathing her in, slamming my lips to hers, I gently cup her cheek. "Bed?"

She nods, and I nudge her towards her room. "Go on then. I'll clean up here."

Her feet pause. "What did you want to talk about?"

"It can wait."

The Crow business can hold off until the morning. And the rest of what I have to say can wait as long as it needs to. I take my time clearing the table, washing out the glasses in the kitchen, putting the bottles into her trash outside. By the time I'm done and stick my head around her door, she's in bed, curled up under soft-looking cream blankets.

Sleepy brown eyes blink at me. Her lips part, and I wait.

Ask me to stay.

Ask me to hold you.

"Thanks, Dom," she whispers. "Goodnight."

My throat feels tight, but I offer her a smile anyway. "Get some sleep."

Her eyes are already closing as I softly close the door. I make my way outside, making sure all the locks are engaged before I turn and take up my post.

When Nicolo and Drew return, I dismiss them with a shake of my head. "I've got it. Go home."

As they melt into the darkness, I settle in for the night.

Nothing gets to Caterina on my watch.

Nothing, and no one.

Caterina

"Again."

Slapping at the treadmill to switch it off, I pin Vito V'Arezzo with my best death glare, the one that makes my Crows piss themselves on the rare occasions I need to use it. Dante's uncle doesn't blink, giving me a steady look as I swear and switch it back on. "You're trying to kill me. This is some fucking bullshit silent assassination plot. Death by running."

I hate running, and he knows it. But Vito just reaches out and turns up the dial, ignoring my swatting hands. "Faster. Your stamina needs work."

"There's nothing wrong with my stamina," I mumble, but shove my headphones back over my ears and pick up the pace until all I can hear is the pounding bass and the thumping of my own heartbeat inside my head.

I don't know why the hell I thought it was a good idea to work my way through at least two bottles of wine the evening before I had an early morning training session with the other heirs, but here we are.

My legs shake, but I swallow it down and keep going, ignoring the views on offer courtesy of the full-length mirrors in front of me.

Luciano and Dante are sparring behind me, fists flying and a whole lot of male flesh on display that I refuse to glance at. Stefano is working on weights in the corner. For a moment, I think I can feel eyes on me, but when I flick my eyes towards him in the mirror, he's focused on his own workout.

Sheer inhuman fucking force of will gets me through the ten-mile stretch, and when I finally collapse, Vito throws a bottle of water at me with a smirk. "Baby steps."

"Fuck you," I gasp, but I take the sealed bottle and drink until the plastic crinkles in my hands. I left my own on the kitchen counter this morning. Distracted by the sight of Dom outside, casually leaning against the steps like he hadn't spent the whole night stood guard outside my damn door.

I didn't look at him as I left. He just fell into step beside me, both of us silent, both ignoring the fucking huge elephant that followed us all the way into the dining hall until I gratefully slid into an empty chair in the middle of the Crows, losing myself in bullshit politics and listening to grievances and absolutely *not* looking in his direction as he slammed a plate of fried food down in front of me to soak up the last bits of alcohol from my night.

I'm regretting the bacon. My throat burns as I take a seat on the floor, stretching my legs out and watching Dante and his uncle. Vito's not that much older than us, and he and Dante joke as they circle each other, Vito pointing out flaws in his technique that I tuck away for future use.

"Morning, little crow."

"Fuck off, Morelli." My tone is on the edge of violence, and he whistles, even as he settles himself down next to me.

"Someone woke up on the wrong side of the bed this morning. Sore head?"

I have my hand wrapped around the finger heading for my side before he gets anywhere near me, bending it back until he swears. "Jesus. I was only joking."

I leave it a few seconds before letting him go. "Don't touch me without my permission."

Luciano hums. "Your statement implies that I may have permission at some point."

Incredulous, I slide my eyes towards him. "How is life in that delusional little world of yours?"

He throws his head back in a deep laugh, drawing the attention of the others. Vito calls out to us as Dante steps away, wiping his face over with a gym towel. "You have breath to laugh, you have breath to fight. Get over here."

"Fucking ace." Luc gets to his feet with a groan. Blinking, I stare at his extended hand.

"I don't think so." I just did a *ten freaking mile* run. They're lucky I haven't vomited on the floor.

"Corvo! You don't get a free pass because you've got a pussy and a hangover," Vito hollers, and Luc grins down at my scowl. "Shall we?"

We shall fucking *not*. Slapping Luc's hand away, I take my time getting to my feet and following him over to the mats. Stefano drifts over to watch as Dante brushes past me and pauses.

"Focus on his left side. It's weaker," he mutters.

"I don't need any handouts," I snap, and his brows dip down into a frown. "Caterina—,"

But I'm already pushing past him, kicking off my sneakers before I step onto the mat. The black plastic coating crinkles under my feet as

Luc stretches opposite me. "Been a while since we did this. Hand to hand?"

My fingers twitch, and I tilt my head towards the weapons table lining the back wall. "If I have to do this, I'd rather make it interesting."

It's been months since I sparred with knives, and I'm missing the feel of them. Vito claps his hands. "Enough talk. Get on with it."

"Some tutor," I mutter. Some tutors genuinely try to help. Vito? I swear the man just wants to see us all bleed. But we both head over to the table, scanning the options before I point to my choice. The pair of thin steel daggers stand out amongst the chunky weaponry. The guns, the axe, even a fucking sword. But knives are the best.

Picking them up, I wrap my fingers around the detailed handles, testing the weight. "These will do."

"In the mood to draw blood, I see." But I can tell he's tempted. I'm the only other heir who will work with knives, the others preferring their guns. But one thing about Luciano Morelli is his appreciation for a well-crafted knife. He picks up the second set, flipping one over and catching it as his teeth flash. "Try not to ruin my pretty face, Caterina."

My snort is loud. "It might teach you some humility."

But the back and forth between us fades as we get into position, Luc kicking off his shoes to bounce lightly on his feet. Vito smacks his hand on the rope in irritation. "This is a fight, not the fucking ballet."

But he hasn't seen us spar before. Not like this. He's only been here a few weeks. Jonno, the previous tutor from the Fuscos – now *he* appreciated knives. I learned a few tricks from him.

"Come on, little crow," Luciano murmurs, his lips curving up. "Dance with me."

I'm already ready, and before the final word leaves his mouth I'm sweeping my right blade up, directly towards his neck. Steel flashes as he pushes himself up to meet me, the knives smashing together less than an inch away from his skin.

"Well, this is cozy," he murmurs. Then he shoves me back, his arms flying as both daggers come at me.

There's no room for muttered insults now. No room for anything but the fluidity of our own movements and the sound of steel as we move around the space, both of us focused intently on the other. Anticipating movements, trying to match it, feeling each other out.

I feint to the right and Luc falls for it as I step directly underneath his arm, one dagger angled perfectly over his pulse. "My point, I believe."

"*Merda*," he snaps. "First and last."

He takes the next point with a well-placed twist that puts his own dagger against my stomach. Vito and the others are silent now, but I can feel them watching. Our breathing becomes labored as the minutes pass, neither of us letting the other gain ground. My arms begin to ache, and I let out a grunt when Luc catches my double thrust by crossing his daggers and twisting them. I nearly lose my grip, and I snarl.

"Such an angry little kitty cat." He smirks, taking his eyes off the game for a split second.

But a second is all I need.

I drop, sweeping out my foot and knocking him off his feet. He goes down like a sack of fucking bricks, and my daggers are crossed at his neck before he can do much more than blink. Straddling him, I lean over, the smirk spreading across my face. "You were saying?"

His head thumps back against the mat as he lets out a breathless laugh. "I concede. You're fucking magnificent."

The raw honesty in his voice takes me aback, and my daggers slacken. The smile slides away from his face, bright hazel eyes meeting mine. And there's no sign of the insolent man I'm used to seeing.

I'm suddenly aware of the lack of distance between us, our faces close together, his body beneath mine. His heat feels like a brand against the inside of my thighs.

My swallow feels loud. Luciano's eyes dip to my throat, as though he's tracking the flex in my skin, tracking every move I make.

And then there's a very male, very obvious cough. I watch as the expression filters away, as Luc carefully wipes at and offers me his usual sly grin. "Feel free to stay there all day, little crow."

It takes me a second longer to collect myself, and a small dip appears between Luc's eyes as I silently pull back my daggers and climb off him. When I offer my hand, he hesitates, and my eyes roll. "It's not a marriage proposal, Morelli."

"More's the pity." But he takes my silent offering, his grip strong as I pull him up. My back turns as soon as he lets go, already heading to place the daggers back on the table as Vito barks new demands behind me. Stefano offers me a nod as I move back to the group, the movement almost congratulatory. But Dante's eyes move between Luc and I, and his jaw tightens as he brushes off Vito's orders. "Session's over."

I check my watch, surprised to see he's right. I head to get my stuff, pulling my sneakers back on and throwing on a sweatshirt to head back to my apartment and change before I see the Crows. Luciano disappears silently, Stefano and Vito leaving together. And then it's just Dante, his gaze burning into my back as I swing my bag on to my shoulder.

"You gonna say whatever it is?" I ask, heading towards the door. "Or do you just enjoy snarling at me from dark corners?"

"Morelli wants you."

My hand pauses on the door handle, and I turn to face him incredulously. "I'm sorry?"

"I said—,"

"No." I hold my hand up. "I heard exactly what you said. But I fail to see how that would ever be any of *your* fucking business – even if it were true."

He holds my gaze. "What if I'm making you my business?"

"Then this—" I gesture between us "—is done, Dante."

"No, it isn't."

Sighing, I reach to pull the door open. "Read the fucking room, V'Arezzo. This was never going to be anything more than temporary. And if you want to act like a fucking caveman, be my guest. But I'm not yours."

His hand lands over mine, shoving the door closed again. "Oh, no. You're not running away from this conversation, *tentazione*. Tell me where you went this summer."

The abrupt change makes my head spin. "I... what?"

"You heard me." Dante steps into me, invading every inch of my space. He presses his face into my hair and takes a deep breath, like he's dragging me into his lungs. "You left. No word from you. The Crows weren't saying anything. That Rossi bastard had them locked up tight. Where'd you go, Cat?"

"None of your business," I manage to choke out. He laughs into me, and his hands are sliding up my arms, slowly pinning my hands to the wood of the door.

"Like I said," he says softly. "I'm making you my business, Caterina Corvo."

One hand keeps my wrists above my head, my chest pushing out towards him. He groans, low in his throat, and his other hand trails down to lift up my face towards his.

"No," he murmurs against my lips. "We're not even close to being done, *tentazione.*"

His kiss isn't soft. Nowhere near. It's a branding, a claiming. His tongue tangles with mine, his lips demanding and firm as his hand cups my throat.

Pushing, always pushing.

I drag my wrists from his grip, wrap my hand around his fingers on my throat and turn us until it's Dante pressed against the door, my hands dragging through his dark hair as our lips duel for dominance. It feels almost too easy as his hands slip down, hoisting my legs around his waist. He breaks away, his teeth threatening my neck until I yank his hair back with an admonishing grunt.

I don't say anything when he flips the lock on the door, sealing us in. I just breathe him in, savoring the taste of his mouth as he walks us back, pressing me down into the mats. It takes seconds for him to yank down my leggings, for me to feel for the hard edges of him, to push his sweatpants down until his cock is hard and hot in my hand. He curses as I swipe my finger over the wet heat of his head.

"Protection," he rasps. "I don't have anything on me."

I pull him closer, my eyes closing. "It's not a problem."

"Thank fuck," he groans, and I tip my head back on a moan as he thrusts into me. He's not gentle, but I don't want gentle. Gentle would feel dangerously close to submission, and that's not what this is.

Gasping, wet sounds fill the room, his muscles rippling in his back and shoulders as I drag my nails over them, reveling in the markings I'm leaving behind. His hand hooks beneath my knee, pushing me up and outwards, hitting me in places that make my eyes roll back in my head.

My hands slide beneath the gray tank thrown on over golden skin. Soaking in the feel of him, the hardness of his chest and the softness of the light scattering of hair covering it. My nail scratches against his nipples and he hisses. "Again."

"No." Just to taunt him, I scratch the barest amount, and he pulls out of me, flipping my body and dragging me up onto my knees. Hot lips press into my damp skin as he pushes back in, his other hand dropping to tweak my clit. "Look at us, Caterina."

My eyes blink open, taking in the two of us reflected in the mirror opposite. Both of us clothed on top, Dante with his fingers on my pussy and one hand under my sweatshirt cupping my breast, rolling the nipple between his fingers in punishment for my teasing. The sight of his cock pushing in and out between my legs is obscene, and my muscles clench around him.

He bites at my neck again, right over the mark he made before. "Don't tell me we don't belong together, *tentazione*. Lie to all of them. Lie to yourself if it makes you feel better, but don't you ever fucking lie to *me*."

He rolls my clit until I cry out, my release hitting like a tsunami, my pussy twitching around him as he thrusts up into me.

I force the words out between gasping breaths. "This isn't permanent, Dante. We are not permanent."

We can't be. He bites my neck again, a silent punishment as I pull my head away. "We could be. If you'd stop fucking *fighting* it, you infuriating female."

It's the teasing undertone in his words, the unspoken assumption that he's going to get exactly what he wants, that makes me snap.

I pull away from him, staggering upright and yanking up my leggings. He sprawls back, full of lazy satisfaction and male expectation.

My hand doesn't shake as I dig into my bag and pull out the Glock. When I turn and point it, the smirk disappears from his face. "Caterina."

My steps are steady. Steady as I walk right up to him, pressing the barrel into the middle of his head as he meets my gaze.

"I am not just a female," I rasp. My throat feels dry, the consequences of my hangover and Dante's grip. "I am a god damned fucking *heir*, Dante. My father is the *capo dei capi*, and one day I will take over from him as leader of the five."

"I know that." His voice is steady. Certain. So certain.

"I can never trust you," I say plainly. When he starts to argue, I shake my head. "For fuck's sake, Dante, you know it's true. We don't live in a world where two heirs can be together. We belong to our families first. I could never trust you not to stab me in the back, and you could never trust me."

Because if I'm ever ordered to put him down, I would do it.

It would kill a part of me, snap away another piece of my soul, but I would do it.

He will always be a V'Arezzo. And I will always be a Corvo.

"I know my duty," I say softly. "It's about time you learned yours. We don't have the luxury of deciding what our future will be, V'Arezzo."

That's something I've already learned, and the lesson was a harsh one. Our fates are already set in stone. Violence, politics, and a shorter lifespan than average is to be expected. But the details, the twists and turns our lives will take? They belong to our fathers. The heads of our families.

Not to us. And every time I look into Dante's eyes, it's another fucking reminder I don't want.

"This is it. Leave me alone," I whisper. The gun is still pressed to his head. "Please, Dante. Leave this alone."

The pain in his face is fleeting, but his eyes harden. "So that's how it is? All that fire in your soul, but you won't raise a single fucking finger to fight for us."

The barb is a direct hit to my chest.

"I am fighting for us." My voice turns icy, as cold as my face when I turn away from him. "And one day you'll understand why."

I leave him there, sprawled on the floor. My heart hurts as I unlock the door, stalking out and across the campus to my apartment.

Shower. Make-up. Hair. Dress.

Building myself back up, again.

Taking those pieces and rearranging them until nobody would notice the pain underneath.

Caterina

I glance down at the dark screen of my phone as some of my senior Crows filter in. Once we're all seated, gathered in one of the rooms allocated to us in the same redbrick building we used to sentence Anton to death, I place it down on the smooth wooden table and look around. "You're all quiet this morning."

Dom catches my eye and subtly shakes his head. Tony, Vincent, Nicolo and Danny are his direct reports. Answerable only to Dom, and through him, to me. Taking the hint, I settle back, letting it slide – for now. "Let's get started."

Dom launches into a brief breakdown of our current activity. Nothing stands out – at least, not until something catches my ear. "The Fusco funds are low?"

Dom flicks through the paperwork in front of him. "They didn't make their last deposit. It was due this week. Could just be an oversight."

My fingers tap on the desk. Establishing the so-called mafia university, a highly exclusive, private educational institution with *significant* tuition fees, comes with several benefits for the five families. One of which is the ability to launder dirty funds through the books, turning it into clean hard cash. Several agreements are in place to make sure all of us benefit equally, but if the Fuscos have stopped paying their share, it's not a good sign.

"I'll look into it." Moving away from Dom, I look at Vincent. "How are the new recruits settling in?"

Short and wiry, Vincent crosses his arms. "Not the worst bunch we've had. That Paul kid is promising."

"Paul Maranzano?" Anton's younger brother. I shouldn't be surprised, given his composure when we did the call, but I wasn't expecting direct praise. Vincent is notoriously difficult to impress.

He nods. "Kid will make a good soldier if he keeps it up."

All of our young men start as *cugines* – junior soldiers. Once they've completed a certain level of training and testing, they move up to become an *associate*. And then, if they're lucky and damn fucking loyal, they get to senior soldier status. Become *Made Men*. Part of the family, like the five men in front of me.

"Watch him. That reminds me, though – I understand the girls are taking part in some new training."

Every single face reddens, except for Dom. He clears his throat. "You know we don't set the schedules."

No, our fathers and their teams do that. All part of preparing the younger generation for the years ahead. "Maybe not, but have any of them mentioned it to you? I don't think it's gone down too well."

They all look blank, and I sigh, tapping my fingers against the table. "We need to consider some sort of representation for the women. As part of the senior group."

It's not something that has come up before. Maybe because we don't actually have that many women here. Many are still kept home by their overprotective fathers. A throwback to the old days, although it's mandatory for the men to attend when they reach eighteen.

Six years of training. We enter at eighteen, and leave at twenty-four, given roles and responsibilities out in the world that our training here prepares us for.

The next year will be my last, and then I'll take on my role in truth, at my father's side.

"Women on your senior council?" Tony asks. There's a touch of sarcasm in his voice, and I turn my face to him slowly.

"What of it?" I ask, tilting my head to the side.

I'm not expecting pushback. Hell, just a look from me most of the time is enough to have any of them shitting themselves. But not today.

He drops his head, but we all catch his mutter. "Guess we're lucky to be told anything at all."

Straightening in my seat, I wait for him to look up. "Explain."

As if realizing where he is, Tony glances around. Nicolo and Danny both stare straight ahead, and he jumps when I slam my hand down on the table. "Now, Tony."

The flush rises on his cheeks, but he lifts his eyes to mine, his mouth twisting. "Did we kill Nicoletta Fusco?"

Well, shit.

I glance around at them all. Considering the tightness in their faces. Buying time to think. "Why do you ask?"

"The other families," Tony mutters. "They're calling us murderers, Cat. Saying we have no honor."

That's news to me. When I glance at Dom, he meets my eyes with a steady gaze.

Guess that answers what he wanted to talk to me about last night.

"Listen to me." When they're all facing me, I choose my words carefully. "What I say now stays in this room for now. I am trying to find out what happened to Nicoletta. But I was not personally involved in, nor did I order her death."

Tony looks relieved. "But that's good news. It means—,"

"It means *Cat* wasn't involved," Vincent says grimly. "But it doesn't absolve everyone."

Danny leans forward. "But you're the *heir*, Cat. Surely you'd know—,"

His mouth snaps shut, and I wonder which of them kicked him under the table. My money would be on Nicolo. Smart kid.

"I am aware of my role," I say drily. "But thank you for the reminder."

When Danny swallows, I sweep my eyes over them. "Something is going on," I say quietly. "I don't know what, yet. But I intend to find out. In the meantime, keep your eyes open. Watch. Listen. Do not engage with whatever shit the others are spewing. They don't know anything for certain, and we're not wasting our energy fighting shadows."

"And if it turns out we *were* involved?" Vincent asks. "That's... not something that sits right with us, Cat. Any of us. What they're saying happened to her... it's fucking barbaric. We don't hurt women and children."

"Present company excepted," Danny blurts, and Dom groans. "Jesus fucking Christ. Remind me why I promoted you, Danny."

Pinching the edge of my nose, I take a breath and pray for patience. "Danny. Shut the fuck up and think before you speak before it gets you into trouble. Vincent - keep an eye on the younger ones and make sure none of them get themselves in trouble or mouth off. Nicolo, Tony, I want you to spread out and listen. See what you pick up. Report back tomorrow."

Standing, I pin them all with a final look. "Remember who we are and to whom we answer. The capo makes decisions based on the needs of the family. Don't assume things when we don't have all the information."

It's a weak end to the meeting, but it's the best I have. Dom follows silently as I storm out, my heels smashing into the gravel as I make a beeline for the apartment. This isn't a discussion for public viewing. "Have you spoken to him?"

"No." My screen is still dark. No call from my father. No fucking contact at all. "This is a fucking punishment, Dom."

"I know." He keeps pace with me as I storm up the metal steps into my apartment. "You expected this."

I head into the kitchen and stop, my hands gripping the sides of the counter. "I expected the cold shoulder. I also expected him to be reasonable enough to separate family and business."

"It's one and the same to him." Dom pushes me into a seat and pulls out my cafetiere. "Coffee?"

"Please." I rest my aching head on the counter with a groan. "What if they're right? If we're responsible for Nicoletta, and I haven't even been *told*—,"

"Then we'll manage it," Dom says simply. A glass of water, condensation dripping down the outside, appears next to me. He drops two painkillers next to it. "Take these."

I swallow them dry, chasing them down with the water. "Thanks. Clearly, I look as shitty as I feel."

When I look up, Dom is leaning against my refrigerator, his arms crossed. "You're pushing yourself too hard. You're exhausted, Cat."

My fingers dig into my temples. "I'm fine. I need to get to my office. I have work to do this afternoon."

He doesn't move. "Reschedule it."

Sighing, I grab my coffee and jump down from the chair, pulling out a flask and pouring the drink into it. "Yes, because when my father is clearly questioning my role as the Corvo heir, the one thing I really need to do is *take it easy*."

When I rip the front door open, I'm not expecting there to be anyone on the other side. Dom pushes in front of me in an instant, blocking my view. "The hell are you doing here?"

"Get out of the way, pup." Dante's voice is scathing. "I'm here for Caterina."

Dom doesn't budge.

"For the love of— *what*?" I lean around him to snap.

My irritation slowly turns to horror when Dante tosses something at Dom. He reaches up to catch it instinctively, and his body locks up.

"You left them behind." Dante raises his eyebrow. "Figured you wouldn't want them left in the training room."

Of course, he couldn't just throw them away. No, he had to bring them here and wave them in front of Domenico like a fucking red rag to a bull.

My hand snaps out, grabbing the black panties from Dom's hands. "Excellent. Thanks for that. Mission accomplished. Now fuck off."

He only smiles, and Dom tenses even more. "Oh, I think I've already hit my quota of *fucking* for the day."

Humiliation creeps across my skin, and something in his face flickers. But Dom steps forward, and his voice is dark. "Leave, V'Arezzo. Before I make you."

The flicker of guilt vanishes. "Such a good little guard dog you are, Rossi. Tell me – does she spread her legs for you as easily as she does everyone else? Or do you just hang around on the edges, waiting for scraps?"

The words take a second to register. To land, stinging my skin like a spray of bullets. But Dom is already moving, his fist snapping out to smash against Dante's face. He staggers back, nearly falling down the stairs before he catches himself against the railings with a grunt.

"Leave," I snap, getting between him and Dom. "Now, Dante."

He spits, blood already seeping from the cut in his lip. "Gladly."

I don't look behind me as I turn to face Dom. His fists are clenched, and his face is pure violence. He doesn't look at me, his eyes focused on Dante's movements. "Domenico. Get inside, now."

It takes a second for him to move, and I push him back through the door, slamming it behind me and tossing the underwear into the trash.

Dom flexes his knuckles. "What the hell do you see in him?"

"I broke it off. He's angry." My words are short. "Again, not that it's anything to do with you."

"He deserved that and more."

Grabbing some ice, I wrap it in a cloth and grab Dom's hand, slapping it on as he hisses. Damn stupid men and their pissing matches.

"Did you tell him?" Dom's voice is low. When I glance up, he's watching me with those piercing, winter gray eyes. He twists his hand, catching mine in his grip before I can turn away.

Silently, I shake my head, and he blows out a breath. "Maybe you should."

I tug my hand, and he releases me. "It wouldn't do any good, Dom."

I can almost taste his disagreement, but he doesn't say anything. Maybe he's just as unwilling as I am to rehash an argument we've had before.

Caterina

Taking a sip of my coffee, I stare out of the kitchen window. Searching for some damn inspiration, trying to sort through the chaos in my head.

I need to work. But I need to speak to my damn father more. Blowing out a breath, I don't turn around as I address Dom. "Change of plans. I'll stay here this afternoon. Send Danny over. I don't want any more unwelcome visitors."

He shifts. "I can—,"

"No." My words are sharp. "You stood outside all damn night. Just get one of the boys here. You need to get some rest, or you'll be no good to anyone, let alone me."

Dom comes to stand beside me. "I'll send two. And I'll check the cameras before I leave. I'm not comfortable with this Fusco business, Cat."

My mouth opens, ready to chastise him for being overprotective. But... he's not wrong. Emotions are running high across the campus. And people make bad decisions when they're not thinking clearly. I'm not about to cut my own nose off to spite my face when it's my safety on the line. "Fine."

The front door clicks shut behind him, and I wait a minute before glancing down to my phone, the screen already lit up.

Lock your damn door.

My lips twitch as I stroll over. I can almost guarantee that he's still standing on the other side, glowering and waiting until he's confident that every lock is secure. I exaggeratedly slap each one into place, making sure he can hear it.

Done. I hope nobody's hiding under the bed.

If they are, shoot them.

Biting back a smile, I take a seat on the couch, resting my head back against the wall and finishing the rest of my coffee. Mentally preparing myself before I reach out and grab my phone.

"Answer the damn call," I mutter. "Come on—,"

"*Cugina.*"

Frowning, I pull the headset away from my ear, checking to make sure I've dialed the correct number. "Matteo. Why are you answering my father's phone?"

My cousin clicks his tongue. "That's hardly a greeting for your favorite cousin, Rina. How is life down at your little school?"

His tone is scathing. Matteo – my only male cousin on my father's side – isn't shy about his opinion on mafia university, despite going through it himself only five years ago. "It's fine. Put my father on the phone."

"Please."

I grit my teeth. "*Matteo.*"

You complete and utter asshole.

He makes a humming sound down the phone. "Actually, I'd like a chat with my little *cugina* first. It's been so long since we spoke last that

I wonder if you've been avoiding me. Anything interesting happening down there on the schoolyard?"

His tone sends a warning down my spine, and I sit back, lips pursing in irritation. "Nothing of interest to you, I'm sure."

He cackles, the sound starting low and getting higher. There's something inherently *wrong* with Matteo. Always has been. But in recent years, his penchant for cruelty has only sharpened under the direction of the Cosa Nostra. My father uses him liberally for wet work, despite my concern that it would only make him worse. He sees him as a guard dog. Leashed. Under control.

There's nothing controlled about him. He's psychotic.

"Oh," he purrs, when his laughter dies down. "I wouldn't say that at all. Not when I had so much *fun* recently. I thought word might have spread by now."

Jesus. My stomach twists. "What kind of fun?"

He hums. "She cried so prettily for me. Bled prettily, too. Such lovely patterns it made, all across my walls. She didn't last very long, though. I didn't expect that. Quite fragile, really."

I have to pull the phone away from my ear, breathing in through my mouth and out through my nose at the image he paints all too vividly.

But his words confirm what I already knew, even as I tried to deny it.

Matteo killed Nicoletta Fusco.

We killed Nicoletta.

He's still fucking talking, lost in his own sick little world. "I put her back together, and I left her for them. What was left of her, at least."

"Put my father on, Matteo. *Now*." I don't want to listen to his shit. Don't want those thoughts of Nicoletta in my head. Nausea sweeps through, climbing up my throat.

She was innocent. Barely a fucking adult.

Not a part of our world, not really.

"Rina," he admonishes. "Your father is a busy man."

"Put him on immediately." My voice lowers. "Or have you forgotten where you sit in the hierarchy, *cousin*? Are you in need of a reminder?"

He goes silent, and I hear what sounds like the snapping of teeth. "For now. Nothing is permanent, Rina. Perhaps it is you who needs the reminder."

Before I can respond, there's a shuffling sound, and my father's voice comes through.

"*Carissimo*. What is it?"

There's no smile in his voice, no fondness despite the nickname. I may as well be any of the men calling in. So I adopt the same tone.

"I need to understand the motivation behind Nicoletta Fusco. Word is spreading here and I need to contain it."

"So contain it." He sounds impatient. "Is that all?"

I blink. "I need to be aware of these things as and when they happen. We don't exist in a vacuum down here, Papa. Giovanni Fusco will return soon, and I need to be prepared when he does."

My father sighs. "I told you that the Fuscos were getting out of line. We handled it."

"By setting *Matteo* on Carlo's eldest daughter?" My voice rises. "That's not handling it, Papa. That's inviting a damn war between the families."

"It's a reminder of who they're dealing with." My father sounds brutal. There's no softness in his voice, no trace of the man who raised me. "This is the world we live in, Caterina. The world you need to embrace. There's no room for sentimentality here, not if we want to stay on top. This is a warning – not just to Carlo Fusco, but to every family, not to put a fucking toe out of line. There are enough enemies outside of the Cosa Nostra, and they're growing every day. The world is changing, and people don't fear us like they used to. If we fight among ourselves, we have already lost. Obedience is paramount, and I have taken steps to ensure it."

"You didn't need to do this," I force out. "There are other ways. You have broken something fundamental to who we *are*—,"

"*I make the fucking laws.*" His voice rises in a shout. "I am the *capo dei capi*, Caterina. Sometimes that comes with difficult choices. That you don't see that is evidence of how much you still have left to learn."

My head jerks back at his condescending tone.

"I was taught," I say slowly, "that we do not hurt the innocent. That is what *you* taught me."

"Well, the world we knew has changed. Decide where you stand, Caterina. I won't have a weak heir stepping up when I'm no longer here. Remember what *you* have at stake."

He may as well reach through the phone and slap me across the face.

My silence is stony, and he sighs. "It's a difficult time, Caterina. Your role is critical. Watch the Fuscos closely. Giovanni Fusco is not the man his father is. Brash, prone to emotion. Carlo understands the message we have sent. Giovanni has been vocal in demonstrating that he does not."

"What do you want from me?" I ask flatly.

"Get him under control. I know that you're not going to disappoint me again, *carissimo*. Am I right?"

I swallow down the lump in my throat. "Of course. I will... handle it."

"If you can't, Fusco has another daughter."

A wave of cold spreads over my body. "Understood. I will handle it."

"Make sure you do."

The call ends, and I slowly bring the phone down from my ear.

There are a dozen things I need to do. More than a dozen. But all I do is sit, frozen.

All I can see is Nicoletta Fusco's face.

All I can hear is my father's voice.

Remember what you have at stake.

I give myself ten minutes. Ten minutes, to let the thoughts threaten to overwhelm my mind. And then I pack them away, piece by piece. My hands no longer shake when I pick up the phone and send a message to Domenico.

Meet me in my office. We have work to do.

DANTE

My eyes lock on to Domenico Rossi as Cat shoves him back through the door. He looks ready to lunge for me again, and I bare my teeth.

Try it, you son of a bitch.

He won't find me such an easy target this time.

His fists clench, but Cat is already slamming the door shut. She doesn't look back, doesn't even glance behind her, too focused on her precious fucking enforcer.

I bite back the roaring in my throat, the red-hot anger that had me storming over here, too full of anger and fury and fucking *hurt* to think about what I was doing until I was spitting vicious words at Caterina and watching them flay her open.

She'll never admit it. Not to me, at least. Maybe to *him*. But I know her tells, even if the stubborn *tentazione* pretends that all we have is fucking sex. And the guilt opens up as I play it back in my head, see the way she flinched, then drew herself upright. Like she expected those blows. Like she *believed* them.

"Fuck!" My fist lands against the tree, and agony shoots up my arm as my hand folds under the blow.

Fucking fantastic.

Snarling, I spit out the blood collecting inside my mouth, spinning on my heel and moving away from her front door before I do something stupid, like kick it down, drop to my knees and tell her I'm sorry.

She doesn't give a fuck. She made that clear when she turned and left me in that fucking room after pressing the barrel of a loaded gun into my forehead. I thought I'd broken down her walls, but she was only making them stronger, even as she writhed on my cock like a damn fucking actress.

My mood hasn't improved when I reach our building, the reddened brick matching the blood on my knuckle as I shove the double doors open. Rocco glances up from where he's waiting, his mouth opening.

"Shut up," I snap, and he closes it again.

For a second.

"What happened?" he asks, following me to the elevator. I slap at the button to take us upstairs to my office, shaking off the agony in my hand. It's not broken.

But fuck if loving Caterina Corvo hasn't done a number on me in the last few days. A black eye, a broken nose, a split lip and now a sprained hand to add to the party.

She's not worth it, I tell myself silently. Ignoring Rocco as we get in and the floor creaks, rising up to the second floor. Even the thought feels wrong.

"Dante," Rocco presses. "What the fuck, man?"

"Nothing," I snap. "Nothing *you* need to know about."

My enforcer just pins me with a look. "Who'd you piss off?"

I grunt as the doors open, heading over and pouring myself a glass of amber from the bar. "Domenico Rossi."

Rocco barks out a laugh as I throw myself down into the chair. "I hope he looks worse."

"I wish," I mutter. "Sit down. You're making my fucking neck ache looking up at you."

He takes a seat opposite me. "Ever think it's time to just move on? Plenty of other girls on campus. She's fucking toxic, man."

Not that many, actually. But it doesn't matter. There could be a thousand girls, a thousand options and the only one I'd see is her.

She's the only girl I've seen since I walked through the gates here at the age of eighteen.

Even then, I could see who she'd become. She stood there, throwing instructions to men twice her age without a qualm, taking charge of the Crows without batting an eyelid. Like she was born to lead.

It took me *five years* of waiting. Of teasing her out. Slowly, slowly, never making any mention of forever. And then, when I finally had her, she fucking *left* me.

Just disappeared. No response to my messages.

And now she's back, those walls are ten times harder to scale than before.

Regret weighs heavy in my chest. Regret that we were born on opposite sides, even if everyone talks about the Cosa Nostra as one big family. Turn it over and our world is teeming with disloyalty, betrayal, death.

I would never betray her. But I don't blame her for believing I would.

Blowing out a breath, I put it out of my head for now. We don't have the luxury of our own feelings, not when we have business to manage. "Run down."

To his credit, Rocco doesn't call me out on my blatant lack of concentration. We discuss the latest intake, who we'll replace now that some of the older crowd is set to graduate, what dynamics are working well and where there are tensions among the V'Arezzo group.

"Good," I say at last. Nothing urgently needs attention. Rocco is an excellent enforcer. I rarely have to get involved with the day-to-day management of the V'Arezzos, instead focusing most of my time outside of the university. The V'Arezzos have a tight hold over the gambling scene of North America, and my father brought me into the business a long time ago, ignoring the guidance that we be kept clear until graduation.

When I check my watch, I dismiss Rocco with a wave. "I'll be there for dinner."

His teeth flash. "Make sure you clean up the blood."

Glancing down to my white shirt, I grimace at the rusty trail. I've got a few minutes to make myself presentable. "Thanks for the reminder."

The call comes through as soon as my laptop is open. Dressed in a fresh crisp white shirt, I sit back in my chair. "Father."

"Dante." Frank V'Arezza is still an imposing man, even in his early sixties. He runs a hand through his salt and pepper hair and smiles, although it seems a little off. The smile slides away as he frowns and leans closer to the screen. "What happened?"

I try not to cringe. "Nothing. Campus politics, but nothing you need to bother with."

My father's glare is one he's perfected since my childhood, and I shift in my seat. "I would ask for more information, but I don't have a lot of time. And there is news we need to discuss."

My attention focuses. "Do you have an update on the Fusco situation?"

He looks grim, but he nods. "Nicoletta Fusco was a hit ordered by Joseph Corvo."

It takes a moment for the words to sink in. Caterina's father. The supposed leader of all five families ordered a hit on a young girl. "But... why?"

It's a move I might have expected from the Asante side. But the Corvos... no, I wouldn't have expected it from them.

My father looks tired. Dark circles sit underneath his eyes. "There is movement, Dante. People are talking about Joseph Corvo. We're losing power and have been for a while. Our grip in North America is weakening by the year. Law enforcement is becoming more of an annoyance. The feds are cracking down everywhere, cutting off revenue streams. There was... some discussion over whether he remains the right man for the *capo dei capi* role. We also heard whispers of some more... unsavory dealings, being made by one of his men. Apparently the rumors were true. As Carlo Fusco has now discovered, to his loss."

He sounds aggrieved, and I don't blame him. My father and Carlo are fairly close. Similar ideals, both of them passionate enough to talk for hours. Ideals that have never quite fitted with Joseph Corvo's old-school vision for the Cosa Nostra.

Concerned, I lean forwards. "If this is a warning, have you put safeguards in place?"

My father purses his lips. "I have no daughters. No wife for him to concern himself with. But I have you. I want you to be careful."

His words are matter of fact, but I can hear the pain underneath. He never remarried after losing my mother in childbirth with my youngest sister.

Two graves for us to visit on holidays. A family cleaved apart.

"I will be careful," I promise.

"Good." His smile is wan. "I can't lose you too."

My thoughts turn to somebody else. "How have the Fuscos reacted?"

"Badly. Corvo has made a severe miscalculation. The Fuscos are ready for war, Dante. And I don't blame them. What happened to Nicoletta... it was a massacre. A violation. There was nothing honorable about it."

He watches me. My father and I are close, closer than most of the other heirs with their own dons, their own fathers. He waits for me to put the pieces together.

"Caterina," I breathe. "They're going after Cat."

He nods reluctantly. "Carlos is angry, but Giovanni is beyond reckoning with. And as an heir, Caterina is seen as fair game, Dante."

Fuck. *Fuck*.

"And if war comes?" I ask, dread tightening my throat. "Which side will we stand on?"

I already know the answer.

"The right one." My father meets my eyes. "I will not stand with a man who butchers the innocent, Dante. Our world is violent enough without that added horror. No matter the reason. I'm sorry."

Meaning that at some point, Cat and I will be on opposite sides. Enemies in truth, and not just in sly, double-edged bickering that ends with us wrapped up in each other.

It means I'm going to lose her.

"Think it over," my father says gently. "I understand more than you might think, Dante. But I cannot – and will not - compromise our principles for the sake of one woman. Caterina has her own choices to make. Whatever she may be to you, she is an heir first. We must treat her as one."

And she will follow her father. Loyalty is the core of who we are. Who *she* is.

The beating of my heart speeds up to a rapid, pulsating rhythm. "I need to go."

"I don't need to remind you to keep our business to yourself." The fatherly concern is replaced by the familiar don. I have no reservations that my father isn't as savage as the rest of them when it comes to business. "But be careful, son. These are dangerous times."

As the screen goes dark, I take a deep breath. First one, then another.

Until my heart settles. Until there's nothing showing of the panic settling into my body, sinking cold claws into me.

And as I walk out into the crisp air, the only part of me showing is the V'Arezzo heir. Cold, calm.

I pass a few of my men as I cross our section of campus, exchanging a few words with each. News of Nicoletta's death is on everyone's lips, but they hold back with the questions in their eyes. I still hear the Corvo name whispered, but they stop short of questioning me directly as I pass the V'Arezzo boundary, striding straight over the common ground into the Corvo territory.

And as luck would have it, the first man I see is exactly who I'm looking for.

I spot him before he sees me, walking along with his eyes on the ground, brow furrowed in that moody bastard way he pulls off like perfection. Pausing, I wait until realization that he's not alone tightens his shoulders and his eyes flick up.

Domenico Rossi pauses, his eyebrows shooting up. "Back for another round, V'Arezzo? What the fuck did I just say?"

But I'm in no mood for fucking around. "I need to speak with you."

He observes me for a moment, taking in the expression on my face, before he tilts his head. "Walk with me."

I don't miss that it's in the opposite direction to Cat's apartment. He takes me back over the boundary line, heading for the neutral ground of the Courtyard, and I scoff. "Please."

"They exist for a reason," he points out. "Otherwise we'd be constantly fighting over ground." We stop in the shade of the oak tree. "Whatever it is you have to say, V'Arezzo, spit it out."

It seems we're both in a similar mood. "Joseph Corvo had Nicoletta Fusco murdered."

I watch him carefully, spotting the tiny jerk of surprise. He covers it well; I'll give him that. But not well enough. He stays silent, waiting me out. Neither confirming nor denying.

Domenico Rossi knows how to play the game, but I'm not here to dance around.

"Listen to me, Rossi," I say quietly. Two Morelli men walk past us, eyeing us and muttering between themselves. "Giovanni Fusco wants blood. His sister is dead, and he wants revenge. There's an easy target for him right here. A double hit. Not just Corvo's heir, but his daughter too. An eye for an eye."

He stiffens, his mouth opening.

"Whatever you think of me," I say, cutting off the words. "We both have the same priorities."

He scoffs. "Don't ever put me and you in the same bracket, V'Arezzo. Cat's nowhere near your list of priorities. She's your fucking current piece, and when you get tired, you'll move on. She deserves better than a piece of shit like you."

"Someone like you, you mean?" He eyes me, so full of resentment and jealousy he's practically burning up with it. "You're so fucking obvious it's laughable, but don't ever assume you know *anything* about my relationship with Caterina."

I don't expect the snort of laughter, the sarcasm. "If you only knew."

Pinching the bridge of my nose, I sigh. "If you two braid each other's hair and swap secrets about your sex lives, that's your call. But there's a fucking *target* on her head, Domenico. The threat is very real. All of this university bullshit they're putting us through? It's the background for *war*. And she's right in the fucking middle of it."

Any amusement wipes from his face. "I'll keep her safe, V'Arezzo. What are *you* going to do? If they come for her, where will you be? Getting in their way, or pushing the knife in yourself?"

My lips press together. The answer should be obvious, but it's not that easy.

Not with my father's words beating a rhythm in my chest. Rossi gives me a grim look, shaking his head. "Didn't think so. Like I said – you don't fucking deserve her. Thanks for the warning. I'll take it from here."

As he walks away from me, I tug down the cuffs on my shirt. "I'll do what I can. That's all I can promise."

Rossi pauses. "If you're not willing to burn the world down for her, V'Arezzo, get out of the way and make room for somebody who will. That's what she deserves. Not a half-assed offer which means fuck all when shit hits the fan."

Deep – *deep* – down, I know that Domenico Rossi is a good man. Maybe he would be the type of man that Cat needs. Someone to stand at her side, without reservation. Without the barriers thrown in our way by virtue of our birth.

"Not all of us have that luxury." My voice is hoarse. "So count your blessings, Rossi."

~~G~~iovanni

The rain is everywhere. Thick, brutal sheets of water hammer our small group from above, as though the sky is grieving with us.

The muted, choking wails of my mother are only just loud enough to be heard over the downpour. They've quietened over the last hour, as though her throat is on the verge of giving up. Raw and broken as she clings to the wooden box, crushing the flower displays someone placed on top.

Nicci was the best of us. Even Rosa would agree. The middle child, the creative one. First to dance in the rain, first to start the singing at our family dinners. First to laugh and first to open her arms for a hug. When she wasn't on the move, she was perfectly still, curled up in a corner with one of her ridiculous romance books.

I can't stop looking in every corner. Hoping for a glimpse out of the corner of my eye. The books remain, some of them dog-eared and pages turned over, waiting for her to return and pick them up again. But my sister will not be coming back.

There will be no more singing. Only the haunting grief of my mother as she holds onto the parts of Nicci we were able to put together for burial.

Some of those parts I collected myself from the lawn of our family's estate. My father couldn't do it, couldn't face seeing his daughter like that. He tried to drown himself in alcohol instead, tried to drown out the sound of my mother's screams as Rosa tried to console her through her own tears and I sent the staff away, slowly making my way outside. I found the softest, silkiest blanket we had in the house, and I picked up the scattered parts of my little sister that the Corvos deigned to leave us.

For the most part, unrecognizable.

For the most part.

My stomach flips, threatening to bring up the coffee I managed to choke down this morning. The priest pauses as he walks past me, instead lowering his head and carrying on. The men stood beside the graveside, waiting to do their work, shift on their feet, casting uncomfortable glances towards the grieving woman unable to let go of her child.

My mouth moves at last, although the rest of me feels frozen. "Leave."

They exchange glances, and one swallows. "Sir...,"

They have a job to do. I hold out my hand. "Give me a shovel, and leave."

The one in charge hesitantly hands it over, the others following behind him as they leave us alone. Rosa looks at me desperately where she kneels next to Mama, her thick auburn hair sticking wetly to her forehead and shoulders, her make-up halfway across her face.

Across from them, my father's gaze is vacant, even as he watches his wife. He can offer no comfort, and my mother wouldn't accept it if he tried. My previously inseparable, loving parents have a jagged crack between them, full of blame and guilt that seems insurmountable.

They did this.

I shove the thoughts away. I will allow no part of them into this space, this final goodbye.

The shovel thuds to the ground as I take heavy steps towards my mother. Rosa is whispering to her, her hand stroking her back in shaking movements.

My hand squeezes her shoulder. "Into the car, Rosie. There are towels. I'll bring Mama."

Wiping at her face, I watch as my youngest – now my only, and the pain spikes at the thought – sister scrambles to her feet. Barely sixteen, but the last of her childhood has been ripped from her. She hugs her arms as she turns away, and I gently slide my arms under my mother.

She fights me, weak as a kitten as I lift her. I don't think she's eaten in days.

"Nicci," she cries. Her hands batter my chest. "I won't leave her here alone. Put me down."

"Rosa needs you," I rasp. "I'll stay with Nicci, Mama. She won't be alone."

My mother slides into rambled mutterings as Rosa opens the car door and I place her inside. The driver already has the heating up, and I grab a towel from the stack I had put in this morning, wrapping it around her. Rosa sniffs, wiping at her face. My mother ignores her, pressing her face against the window.

"Take them home," I order Santo. "Make sure my mother gets inside the house."

Then I turn back to Rosa, my eyes skipping over my mother. "I won't be too long."

She nods, already lifting my mother's freezing hands and rubbing them gently. "Don't... don't rush, Gio."

They pull away, leaving me with my silent father and my dead sister.

His footsteps tread behind me as I pick up the soaking wet rope. He takes the other side, and together we lift Nicci into the dirt, lowering her gently, so fucking gently, down into the cold, packed earth.

She doesn't belong here. The wrongness of it jars against my chest, a physical pain that I haven't been able to shake in the days since I arrived home to my father's call.

As the coffin touches the bottom, the rope slacking in our hands, my father drops to his knees as though he's a puppet, his strings slashed. He buries his face in his hands as I move around him, picking up the shovel.

It shakes in my hands, but my grip is firm as I press my foot into the sharp edges and push down, filling it with soil that thumps wetly over the final resting place of Nicoletta Fusco.

A daughter.

A sister.

And as she disappears under the dark mountain of dirt, I make her a promise.

I will make them pay.

CATERINA

I take my time getting ready, using the minutes to pick through the myriad of thoughts wrestling for space inside my head. Mindful of the current atmosphere on campus, I select black, fitted leather trousers, sliding my feet into my custom crimson heels. I have them made every year as a gift to myself, with a little added *extra*.

The thin steel daggers, ornately carved with engraved wooden handles, slip perfectly into place, sliding into the sheath at the back of each heel. Easy to reach if I need them, but they look fucking phenomenal even if I don't.

Adding a second pair to the thin wraps strapped to the underside of my arms, I slip on a black satin camisole and my holster, adding two Ruger-57s and covering them with a fitted blazer.

With my hair scraped back, away from my face, my eyeliner in a perfect flick and my lips painted to match my shoes, I look ready.

Ready to kill, or ready to fuck.

I was taught a long time ago that my appearance is a weapon in itself, and I'm not a fool. I'll use every weapon at my disposal if I need to.

And it's the look that counts. Especially today, as the whispers dog my footsteps through the campus. I keep my head high, maintaining eye contact with anyone brave enough to try to stare me out.

Nobody dares for longer than a few seconds. Even my own Crows give me a wide berth, and Vincent catches my eye as he corrals a handful of junior soldiers towards the training rooms. They all gawp, before he smacks one in the back of the head and they stumble inside.

Dom is already waiting when I arrive, leaning against the brick wall. He scans me as I walk up. "You already know."

"Inside."

Dom does a sweep of the room first before locking the door and crossing his arms. "Fucking hell. It's true, isn't it?"

Unbuttoning my blazer, I hang it over the back of my leather chair. "It is. Who told you?"

For him to be so certain, the source must have been a good one. When he hesitates, my suspicions rise. "Domenico."

His chin tips up. "Dante V'Arezzo."

My lips part. Dante left my apartment barely an hour ago. "He came back?"

Dom nods. "He wanted to speak to me. Gave me the heads up."

Leaning back in my seat, I tap my fingers in a rhythm on the desk. "Did you have fun discussing my protection detail without me?"

There's no remorse in his eyes when he meets my gaze. "He passed on the information, and that's it. That discussion is for us to have. The Fuscos aren't going to mess around, Cat. They want blood. And yours would send the best message."

I tap the guns strapped to my body. "I'm not unaware. And I don't plan to be unprepared."

"You can't hold them all off," Dom points out. "I'm putting a rota on you, twenty-four seven. Four guards, swapped in and out."

"We don't have the senior headcount for that." There are thirty-eight Crows on campus and only twelve have senior soldier status, not including me and Dom. The Fuscos have a little more than that.

"I'll speak to Aldo, see if he'll send some men down here for cover."

"He won't." My eyes drop. "My father expects me to handle this."

"Then we'll add some of the more promising juniors to the rota. It'll be experience for them, and I'll pair them with a senior." His face is uncompromising. "I'm not fucking around here, Cat. You're taking the guards."

I hate having eyes on me at all times, and he knows it. "That's not a permanent solution."

"No," he agrees, leaning forward. "So, what's the plan?"

I can already feel the beginning of a headache. Rubbing my temples, I talk him through the conversation I had with my father. "I need to get a handle on Giovanni. And he's not a man to be reasoned with at the best of times. For now, we wait. He's not even here yet. I don't want to make a move that pushes him in a direction he might not be planning."

"That puts us on the back foot. I don't like it."

I glance up at that. "That's the order, Dom. We watch, and we wait. I'll take the guards. Let's see what frame of mind he's in when he gets back."

Dom's phone rings, and he lifts it to his ear. I stare out of the window, watching the birds outside. The pounding in my head deepens. When he finishes, I glance over to him. "Looks like we didn't have long to wait after all."

His hand tightens on the phone. "His car just pulled in through the gates. I don't think you should go to the dining hall tonight."

Sighing, I open my laptop. "I'm not hiding, Dom. We're not weak, and he's not going to start a war in full view of everyone. My orders hold."

He doesn't move.

"Go and sort the rota." My voice is firmer this time. "I've got a financial law lecture in an hour, and I'll go to the dining hall from there. Make sure the guards are in place. Hell, walk me there yourself if it makes you feel better. But that's the plan."

Gray eyes sweep my face. "Fine. Just... be careful, Cat."

My fingers rest on one of the guns, my words grim. "I'm always careful."

And if I can't be careful, I'll be *fast*.

Hopefully fast enough to outmaneuver whatever trouble is heading my way.

Caterina

It's not nerves that churn my stomach as I head into the dining hall, but irritation. I'm late, held up by the rambling Morelli law tutor who decided to spend the whole session running over old ground instead of teaching us anything new. One of the disadvantages of constantly swapping out the teaching staff.

My shoulders are back, my stride confident as two of the men that appeared this afternoon leap to pull the double doors open. When I sweep through, heads start to turn in my direction. The buzz of low-key dinner conversation ends in an abrupt wave, spreading out from the table closest to me until it reaches the head table.

A brief scan tells me Giovanni Fusco hasn't arrived yet. Only Luciano and Dante are there, both of them watching me closely, taking in the outline of the guns strapped to my body.

But the Fusco table is full, fury pouring off them in silent waves as I stalk past. Leo dips his head to listen to the muttering girl next to him, his lip curling. He doesn't look away from my stare, doesn't back down. The men around him almost vibrate in their anger, their hands fisted. Hatred oozes from them, so strong I can almost taste it on my tongue.

It's an explosion waiting to happen. Across from them, the Crows are silent. Watchful. Waiting for a signal. For a spark. Domenico only stands once I'm past the Fusco table, his shoulders tight as he heads over to the serving tables. I don't wait, the click of my heels loud in the silence as I ascend the steps. Luciano and Dante are deathly still as I walk around them, yanking out a seat and dropping into it.

It feels as though the room is holding its breath. Nobody is eating, every person watching us. Domenico is the only movement as he jumps up the steps and places a full plate in front of me. His face tips up in a crooked smile. "Steak. Your favorite."

"Smells good." With a returned smile, I wait for him to return to his seat before picking up my cutlery and digging in, ignoring every single fucking one of them.

"Playing with fire, Caterina." Luciano sounds amused, but there's an edge to his voice. If violence erupts in this room, no family will escape unscathed.

I take my time, swallowing my food before I respond in a louder tone. "I'm just eating my dinner, Morelli. I didn't realize my eating habits were so... *interesting*."

My words carry into the silence, and there's a clatter as the Crows pick up on my not particularly subtle annoyance. Slowly, the Morellis follow their lead, then the V'Arezzos, until the only table still silent is the Fusco group.

Dante's voice is low and hard. "You shouldn't be here."

My head turns to him slowly, taking in the state of his face. The tiniest hint of guilt works its way in, but I push it down. I have too much going on to worry about something that he caused. "Do we have to have the conversation about what is – and *isn't* – your business again? It didn't work out too well last time."

"Cat—,"

"He's not wrong," Luc's voice is softer, and when I turn to him, he's staring down at me. "This is dangerous, Caterina."

Ignoring them, I take another bite of my food. "I won't hide," I say finally. "It only delays the inevitable."

"Which is your head on a fucking platter," Dante hisses. "They're not fucking around, Cat."

"Neither am I," I say shortly. "They won't move until Gio arrives. If we need to fight, me and mine are ready. Get your people out if you're concerned."

Luciano curses. "Too late for that, little crow."

As I look up, I hear the first bang.

One.

Then another.

Leo lifts his fist again, his eyes on me as he slams it against the table.

Again.

The girl next to him lifts her chin and does the same.

Bang.

Bang.

Bang.

The whole table takes up the silent chant, each bang reverberating through the room. Dom gets to his feet, heading straight for me, every single one of the Crows going on alert as the men on either side of me tense.

And then, as if on cue, the banging stops.

The doors fly open.

And Giovanni walks in.

There's nothing casual about his movements as he walks between the tables. He doesn't spare a glance for his own table. No, his gaze is directed elsewhere.

Directly at *me*.

And there's so much hatred in his indigo blue eyes, sheer hate and fucking *pain* that I nearly drop my gaze before I steel myself.

There is no room for my shame or guilt here. Not when a single wrong move could cost any of us our lives.

Later. Later, there will be time to self-flagellate. For now, I have to be a Crow.

The Crow.

I am Caterina Corvo, and I am a Crow.

Dom moves into his path, blocking any view of me, and Gio stops, breathing heavily. Behind him, a young girl walks in, and Leo beckons her over to their table. She looks at me with an expression identical to her older brother as Leo wraps his arm around her shoulders protectively.

Rosa Fusco.

Silence again.

"Get out of my way, Rossi."

Gio's tone is colder than I've ever heard it. As though he's taken the fire that has fuelled him ever since I've known him and converted it to pure ice. It coats every word as Dom draws himself up. "You're not touching her."

"Domenico." My voice is quiet, but Dom jerks at the soft admonishment as though I've struck him directly between the shoulder blades. "Let him pass."

"Do as your master says, dog." Scathing words. "This is an heir matter."

For a moment, I don't think Dom will move. His head twists around, and my gut clenches at the look in his eyes. His hands flex, stretching out, before he shifts to the side. "Touch her and I will *kill* you, Fusco."

"I invite you to try."

My hands grip the table, and I force them to loosen. Beside me, I don't think Luc or Dante are even breathing. Dante angles himself towards me, and I shake my head minutely as Gio glides up the steps, stopping with the table between us.

He looks older, heavier, than when I last saw him. The grief of losing his sister weighs on him, showing in the black smudges under his eyes. His hair is longer now, still curled on top but shaved on the sides to try and keep it in check.

"Giovanni." I settle casually back in my seat, letting him stand there. "I heard you had returned."

Eyes everywhere. So many eyes, watching us. I would have preferred privacy for our first meeting, and when his lip curls up in a cruel mockery of a smile, I realize he knows that.

"I have. We buried our sister yesterday. The parts of her you left us, anyway."

The words are sharp, a direct attack. They hit me hard. "Gio, I—,"

"Don't you dare," he interrupts. The agony spreads across his face. "Don't you fucking sit there and try to tell me you're *sorry for our fucking loss*."

Fuck. Fuck, *fuck*.

Have to play the game.

"I was going to say," I keep my words light, mild. "That I hope Rosa settles in well. A little young, but we'll let it slide. All things... considered."

It's a fucking cheap shot. A shot, and a threat. But I have to shut him down. My father has already shown that he has no mercy where the Fuscos are concerned.

Don't push this anymore, I beg silently. *Don't make this any worse, Gio.*

There's a hissed insult from the room that I'm certain comes directly from the youngest Fusco. Gio's eyes flicker.

And then he smiles.

I smooth away the confused crease in my brow as he smirks. He takes a step forward until his body is pressed against the edge of the table.

"I have a gift for you, Caterina Corvo." His voice lifts, carrying across the room in a clear challenge. "Stand up, so I can give it to you."

I stay in my seat, and he crosses his arms. "Scared, Crow? If it helps, I swear not to harm you until this discussion is over."

Slowly, I stand.

Dom hovers to the side of us, still and coiled in readiness if Giovanni puts even a foot wrong. My hand slides into my holster and Gio traces the movement, letting out a caustic laugh.

"You won't be needing that."

And then he *kisses* me.

Caterina

The barrel of my gun presses into his stomach, my finger steady on the trigger as he brushes his mouth against my lips. Once. Twice. The stubble on his face is edging towards a beard, and it scrapes against my skin. Gio's mouth curves, and then he pulls back.

The kiss was softer than silk, but all I feel is cold. Colder than the feel of his lips against mine.

My eyes move to Domenico. He's paled, one foot on the steps. But he can't do anything, can't change what's just happened.

Nobody moves. Nobody dares to even breathe.

Nobody, except for Giovanni. He straightens the lapel of his sleek black suit jacket as he turns away from me.

"No guns. One on one only," he announces. The rules settle into my skin. And then he turns back to me, one more time. "I want you to feel every second, Caterina. Just like Nicoletta did."

Il bacio della morte.

The kiss of death.

A bounty on my head, for anyone brave enough to try.

Giovanni Fusco has just declared open season on my life.

Wherever I go, I will be hunted.

As one, my senior Crows are up, flowing in solid movement as they form a line between me and the tables. Dom is up on the platform in the next instant, his voice hoarse. "Orders."

But all I can do is stare at Gio, as he strolls around and pulls out the empty seat on the side of Luciano, dropping into it as though he hasn't just detonated a bomb over my head.

"Cat." Dom's voice wavers, his head twisting as though people are going to start launching weapons in my direction. "*Orders.*"

Slowly, I wet my lips. Glance down to the heirs on either side of me. Dante is nearly as pale as Domenico. Luciano glances between Giovanni and I, his brow creased.

I wonder where Stefano is. When Dom grabs my arm, it snaps me out of the treacle of panic hazing over my mind.

"Sit down, Dom," I whisper. He starts to shake his head, and I reach around for my seat. "I *said*—," my voice hardens. "Sit down. I haven't finished my food."

I look at the Crows. "All of you. Stand down."

Vincent turns his head, incredulity in his gaze.

Dishes rattle as my hand smashes into the table. "*Now!*"

My roar echoes through the room, propelling them into action. Dom ignores me, moving to stand directly behind my chair.

"Try to move me," he grits out when I begin to turn. "I swear to fucking god I will carry you out and *fuck* the hierarchy."

Fine. I drag my plate towards me, stabbing my fork into the cold meat. It tastes like death in my mouth, but I force myself to chew, to swallow, to sip at my drink as if there isn't a group of people actively plotting my death in the same room.

I eat every bite.

When I finally place the cutlery down, there's a collective sigh of relief both behind and to the sides of me.

"Thank fuck," Dante mutters. "*Now* will you leave?"

I take a moment to check the positioning of my weapons before I stand. Dom is there, ready to guide me through the small exit to the side, but I dodge his outstretched hand and wind around the table, ignoring his frantic curse.

More eyes, as my heels stab into the floor. The Crows are half out of their seats, uncertain and worried as their heads swivel around the room. Amie looks petrified as her head darts around, looking for threats.

But only one person gets up.

I pause as Rosa Fusco ducks under Leo's arm, darting into my path. I hold my hand up to stop any of mine getting involved. Her eyes are lighter than her brothers. A bright, vivid, electric blue that she pins on me.

"You killed my sister."

She can't be more than sixteen. I keep my hands relaxed at my sides as I survey her. "I did not stop it from happening."

Her face twists, like she's trying to hold back tears. "She didn't do anything to you. She never did anything to everyone."

I take a breath. "Sometimes," I say quietly, "bad things happen to people who do not deserve it."

The girl considers my words. She nods.

And then she draws her head back, and spits in my face.

My head jerks back as she hisses. "You deserve everything bad. I hope you die screaming."

"Rosa." Giovanni's voice is a whip, and she shrinks back, darting away to the table as I raise a hand to my face and wipe off the evidence of her hatred.

Nobody else moves as I walk out.

Too busy planning their approach to waste it on a half-assed try.

The cool air hits my face, and Domenico is there. His hand shakes as he uses his sleeve to wipe off the last of it and I push his hand away. "Don't. It's fine."

"This is not fucking fine," he snaps. "This is the furthest thing from fucking fine, Cat!"

He grabs my arm when I turn. "Where the hell are you going?"

"Home."

He shakes his head in disbelief. "There's a fucking target on your head. You're not going back there."

My feet move anyway. "You chose that spot because it was easy to defend," I point out. "So get the guard duty in place. They're not chasing me out of my home, Dom. I know that space like the back of my hand. I'm just as safe there as I am anywhere else."

More so. There are so many security measures in place, it's locked up tighter than fucking Alcatraz. The only person who's ever gotten past is Dante, and I can't see him stabbing me for the glory.

Although maybe he would, after the last few days.

Domenico follows me, his eyes constantly moving as we head swiftly towards the apartment and up the steps. I only notice my shaking hands when I try to unlock the door.

Warm hands close over mine. "Steady," Dom murmurs. "I'll do it."

For once, I don't argue, stepping back and wrapping my arms around myself. The dark night is closing in, the last of the autumn sun setting over the copse of oak trees. Wind whistles through the clearing, and I glance around.

Phantom eyes watch me, and I flinch when Dom lays his hand on my arm. "Cat."

His touch is gentle as he steers me inside, nudging me down on the couch and disappearing into my bedroom. I blink when he comes back out with a blanket. "What's that for?"

"For you." He wraps it around my shoulders. "You're freezing."

I didn't notice.

Dom moves around my apartment in familiar steps, making coffee. Both of us are quiet, but I notice him glancing out of the window. I wrap my hands around the familiar warmth when he hands me the cup. "Thanks."

He settles down next to me. "This... this could be a shitshow, Cat."

I take my time, sipping at the steaming liquid. "Maybe I should just give up now."

He nudges me. "Not even a little bit funny."

Swallowing, I place the cup down and tug the blanket around me. The solid weight of my guns press into my stomach. "They're going to come, Dom. They'll keep coming, wearing me down piece by piece. Eventually, someone's going to get through. It's inevitable."

I could be in class. Working out. Eating my fucking breakfast, and they'll come. With knives, or poison. All of them trying to fulfill *il bacio della morte*. It might not even be a Fusco. Giovanni will reward anyone who completes it, Fusco or not.

A thought occurs to me. "You can't taste my food anymore."

"Like hell I can't," he says instantly. "This is exactly the reason why I've always tasted your food."

He's done it for six years, always insisting that I couldn't be too careful. I just scoffed and let him get on with it.

Never imagining that it could truly happen.

"I... I don't want to lose you." The words nearly stick in my throat, dangerously close to a confession.

Maybe it makes me weak to need another person as much as I need him.

But at least I'm strong enough to admit it.

When I glance up, his face is grave, gray eyes swirling. "You think I'll ever leave your side, Caterina Corvo? They'd have to put a bullet in my skull first."

I close my eyes. That's exactly what I'm afraid of.

"You're my best friend, Dom." My voice drops to barely a whisper. "I can't do this without you."

Domenico Rossi is woven so tightly into the threads of my life that I have no idea who I would even be without him. Harder. Colder. Dom gives me the shelter to be human in a world that keeps trying to strip every part of humanity away from me.

His hands cover mine. When my eyelids crack open, he's on his knees in front of me.

"I'll always be your best friend," he breathes. "That's never going to change, Cat. Not ever. But *you*—,"

He searches my face, looking for something.

"You are my endgame, Caterina Corvo. And I'm fighting for forever. So you don't get to just *give up*. You want to fall apart? I'll catch you every damn time and put you back together. But you do not get to give up on me. If you're not going to fight for yourself, then fight for me. *Please*."

I lose every particle of oxygen in my body. "Dom..."

He shakes his head, his words a rasp. "Don't act like this is news to you, Cat. We both know it's not. And I'm not asking for anything you're not willing to give."

He looks down. "But I'm *here*. I'm not going anywhere. Don't ask me not to put you first. It's never going to happen."

My eyes start to burn. "I..."

I don't know what to say.

Or maybe the issue is that I have too much that I want to say. But none of it comes out, and Dom sighs. He leans forward until our foreheads are resting together, and I breathe in his familiar scent, sucking it down like it's the oxygen he just stole from my lungs.

"What now?" I ask, and he pulls his head back. The vulnerability I glimpsed a moment ago is wiped away, replaced by his familiar no-nonsense expression.

"Now, you're going to get changed, relax and watch some of that truly shitty reality TV you enjoy." He gets to his feet, and I stare up at him. My head feels like mush.

"What are you going to do?"

"I'm going to make sure no fucker gets to you in here." Leaning down, he brushes a soft kiss across my forehead. "Take tonight, Cat. I've got this. And tomorrow, you can rip them all apart."

Kicking my heels off, I stretch and pad across the room to my bedroom door. "I wish it was that easy."

If only it were as easy as fighting an enemy. The bad guys versus the good. But as the shower pelts down hot water on my back, I can't shake off the look in Gio's eyes. Like he's seen something that's changed him, fundamentally. That's broken him.

His hatred is valid. My father is responsible for the death of his sister. And Matteo would have made sure it was not a swift one.

We are not the good guys. The Corvos are the enemy.

Nausea surges, and I heave over the drain as my dinner makes a reappearance.

What would any of us do for the ones we love?

Whatever happens to me now, more death is inevitable.

And I'm so tired.

I've spent my entire life within the Cosa Nostra. Raised to lead, to take up my father's mantle when he's gone. I have always been proud to be a Corvo, held my head high as a Crow.

But this is not an inheritance I want. One where we butcher the innocent to cling on to the last vestiges of times gone by, to claw our way to power by whatever means necessary.

As the last remnants of my own guilt washes away down the drain, I turn the water off and step out, wiping away the steam covering the mirror. The exhaustion shows in my face. The creases at the corners of my eyes. The dark smudges that only deepen.

"I don't have a choice," I whisper. My father has made that clear over recent months. If I balk - if I *fail* - he will take everything from me.

I have to win.

Domenico

A creaking sound sends my head shooting up. I've been sitting here for hours, watching Cat toss and turn in her sleep on the couch. I should wake her up, get her to bed, but I don't have the heart, not when she's running herself into the fucking ground.

And now this.

Il bacio della morte.

The Kiss of Death. Rarely given, and never escaped. Not in my lifetime, at least.

Slowly, I ease myself to my feet. I'm not worried about them getting in. But there are four Crows out in that clearing, and if they've made it past all four, then either my men are dead or this is someone with more skill than just a made man trying to make a name for himself by taking out the Corvo heir.

Not on my fucking watch.

My gun is solid in my hand as I tread softly to the door. I know every inch of this place, tested the floors myself, and my steps are silent as I pull out my phone, opening up the security app for Caterina's apartment and flicking through the cameras as a text from Danny pops up.

Cursing, I pull the door open. "Jesus fucking *Christ*, V'Arezzo. You're just begging me to put a bullet in your head at this point."

Dante's head is tilted back against the railing, his eyes closed and legs out in front of him. The Glock he favors sits in his lap. "Always a pleasure, Rossi."

"This is not the time," I keep my voice low, not wanting to disturb her. "In case you hadn't noticed, we have a situation here."

His eyes open slowly. "I know. I had a front-row ticket to that little shitshow."

Something in the sarcastic comment doesn't fit. After a moment, I kick at his legs. "Move over."

It takes him a moment, but I settle myself opposite him. There's a whistle from the trees, and I whistle back. "Tell me why I shouldn't whip the fucking lot of them for letting you past."

He huffs. "I'm not giving them a free pass. My men wouldn't let you within twenty meters of my door."

"Would the same apply to Cat?"

He sighs at the implicit question. "Like I said before, Rossi. Regardless of your highly personal and quite frankly *offensive* opinion of me, we do have similar priorities. I have no wish to see Caterina taken out because of her father's actions."

"So what?" I ask, staring at him. His eyes gleam in the darkness. "You offering yourself up for bodyguard duty?"

His jaw tightens, and even I can see the frustration on his face. "I'm limited in what I can do. Not all of us have the freedom to follow our own path. But I won't hurt her, Domenico. And I can give the time I have. You try and cover her twenty-four seven and you'll make mistakes. She can't afford any fucking mistakes."

My head tilts. "And would this be a Corvo-V'Arezzo alliance? I don't have the authority to sign off on that shit."

"No." His voice is hard. "Consider this a personal offer. My father and Carlo Fusco are close."

Slowly, I nod. "I see."

His tone is bitter, and I can understand why.

"You love her."

He gives me a disbelieving look. "The fuck? You really do braid each other's hair, don't you?"

But he doesn't deny it. After a minute, he sighs.

"That's the issue, isn't it? We all fucking love her. Me. You. Even Luciano has started sniffing around. That woman is a ball of fire and fury, and we're all drawn to it like moths to a flame. But none of us can have her."

"Speak for yourself," I mutter. My attention is caught by the mention of Morelli, but then Dante laughs, low and sarcastic.

"Joseph Corvo will *never* let you near her." His words are swift, brutal. "Caterina Corvo will not be given to a mere enforcer, Rossi. And you damn well know it. One day, you'll have to stand back and watch as he gives her to someone else. Wrapped up in a pretty bow. She's a golden opportunity for him, and who the fuck wouldn't give up a piece of their empire for the chance to own her?"

I stay silent.

"Unless... Caterina takes over sooner rather than later." He eyes me, but I'm not giving away a single thing. "Then it'll be up to her who she takes on. As a husband... or a lover."

"She's not a damn possession," I snap. He waves his hand towards his battered face.

"I know that. All too fucking well. But that's not how the old guard sees it. She might be an heir, but she's a female too. That's a fucking enticing package. Add in Caterina herself, and men would go to war for her."

Men would go to war for her.

"Just look at us," he continues, his words soft in the dark night. "You think I'm a whoring, untrustworthy asshole. I happen to think you're a sanctimonious prick. But here we are, having a civil conversation in the name of keeping her safe. If that's not a fucking bad omen, I don't know what is."

The sound that slips out might be amusement. Maybe.

"So," I say. My eyes survey the ground below. "Temporary allies, then. For her."

"For her," he agrees. "Get some sleep, Rossi. I need to leave before dawn. You have my word that nothing will get past this door."

I don't ask what he'll do if a V'Arezzo turns up.

But it occurs to me, as I stand and hold out my hand, that maybe he's not entirely the asshole I thought he was. His shake is firm, and I wonder if he feels the same.

War makes for strange bedfellows, indeed.

The door clicks behind me, and I stare across at Caterina. She still sleeps, that little frown creasing her forehead that never seems to smooth out deepening as I lean down to slide my arms underneath her.

She jerks, her eyes opening.

"Just me," I murmur. "I'm taking you to bed."

But she's already curling herself into me, soft breaths against my shoulder as I carry her into her bedroom, tucking her into bed.

As I flick off the lamp, her hand reaches out. Soft fingers brush my wrist. "Stay."

Her eyes are shut. She might even be dreaming, and if she is, I doubt it's of me. Maybe him, the man sat outside with his gun held close.

But I'm a selfish bastard, and I'll take every piece of her I can get. So I toe off my boots, moving around the bed and setting my gun down on the table before I carefully climb on. Caterina shifts back, burrowing herself against me until all I can feel is the heat from her body, even through my clothes and her silky pajamas.

She sighs as my arm settles around her, and I carefully, so fucking carefully, reach out and brush away the stray hairs covering her face.

She sleeps all night in my arms.

And I don't sleep at all.

Caterina

The silence at breakfast is... awkward.

I pick up another piece of apple, snapping off the end with irritation as I scan the faces around me. Directly across the table, Amie offers me a wan smile before she goes back to staring at her toast.

It could be to do with the men standing around us, forming a wall between the Corvos and the other tables that Dom refused to back down on. Or it could be the death sentence hanging over my head.

All the Crows are twitchy this morning.

"For Gods' sake," I finally snap, when Rico fumbles his cup and coffee spills out in a dark stain over the pristine white tablecloth. Everybody jumps, and it only annoys me more. "We are *Crows*. Act like it."

Muttered apologies come from around me, but the faces are still solemn. Watchful.

And in one case, *angry*.

My eyes land on Paul Maranzano. He's staring at me, his mouth twisted and eyes narrowed. The anger fades away as I stare him out, but I can still see it. "Something to share with the table, Paul?"

The small amount of noise stops altogether. Faces turn towards us, waiting to see what the brother of the traitor has to say.

"I thought being a Crow was honorable." His words are short, sharp as he spits them across the table at me. "Thought that honor came above all else. But apparently, I was wrong."

Behind him, Vincent's eyes drop to his charge. He starts to move forward, face set in lines of fury, but I hold up my hand to stop him.

Paul looks down, but he's not finished. "Everyone is talking about the Fusco girl. They say we butchered her. Carved her up and left her in pieces on their lawn. Where is the *honor* in that?"

Jaw firming, he looks up at me. "Why is my brother *dead,* if none of it matters?"

Eyes move to me. Waiting. Judging.

Paul is not the only angry one. It's in the tight lines of their mouths, the hunched position of their shoulders. And I sit back, assessing.

In our world, where violence and death is so common, having a code of honor is the same as having solid ground. It keeps us in check, reminds us that there are limits to power. Reassurance. Safety. An understanding that no matter how bad things get, there are always lines that we will not cross.

My father has ripped that safety apart. Left me here to pick up the jagged pieces.

And I have no idea what to say to Paul. To any of them.

Not when I agree with them.

"It is not our place to judge when we don't have all of the information." I look around, making sure to meet their eyes. Most of them drop away. "And we don't have all of the information because it is not our *place* to know."

A few nods. Faces turning away.

But Paul isn't ready to let it drop. "Did you know? Did you agree with it?"

A dozen responses form on my tongue. In the end, I choose the truth. "No. I didn't know."

It doesn't absolve me, not as the heir. My father's choices are mine to bear. It also makes me look weak. But a relieved look comes over Paul's face, and I can't bring myself to regret the words.

"Believe me when I say that I regret the loss of Nicoletta Fusco more than you know," I say quietly. "In the days to come, our honor will be more important than ever, Paul. Do not let that line slip away. Hold onto it with everything you have. Humanity is not so easy to reclaim, once it's gone."

He nods, the anger fading into grief as he sits back. But a new rash of whispers breaks out. Dom slips into the seat next to me. "Drawing a line, Cat?"

"An accidental one." Frowning, I push my chair back. I gave away more than I should have in my response to Paul. If I'm not careful, the Crows could split down the middle, at the exact time when I need us to be stronger than ever.

The wall splits, everyone heading off to start their day. Four of the Crows peel off, forming a loose circle around Dom and I as we leave the hall. I glance behind me, wondering if Amie will come to speak to me, but I don't see her in the crowd.

Thankfully, there are only a handful of Fuscos present, and no Giovanni, Leo or Rosa. They glare but stay seated as we walk out. One cocky fucker clicks back an imaginary gun and aims it at me. Smirking,

I slide the knife from my sleeve, twirling it over in my fingers, my skin dancing dangerously close to the sharp blade.

He drops his hand and fucking fast.

"Quiet so far," Dom murmurs, and I poke him in the stomach as we head out. "Don't get used to it."

They will come. *Il bacio della morte* is not to be rushed. It's to be savored, until the victim is worn down by fear and terror just as much as the actual attempts on their life.

It's a mental execution, just as much as a physical one.

I will not allow that to happen.

Checking my phone, I scan the schedule for the day. It's surprisingly full, and I groan. "Law, *again*. God, that tutor is an ass."

Dom grins. "Can't break the law if we don't know the law."

Semantics. He stays next to me as I walk through the door, and I glance at him as I slide into a seat in the middle of the room. He only raises his eyebrows before he drops into the seat next to me.

"Seriously?" Shaking my head, I pull out my laptop. "Biggest regret of your life. Just wait."

"I regret nothing where you're concerned."

My hand twitches, and the laptop nearly slides off the edge of the table before it's caught by a large pair of tanned hands. "Good morning, little crow. Still alive, I see."

Luciano throws himself down into the seat next to me, ignoring Dom's glare. "This is exciting. Three hours with the bat."

"Relative of yours?" I ask sweetly, and he grunts. "My mother's second cousin. Or something."

The old woman slips in through the door, her eyes landing on the three of us and widening as though she didn't expect us to be here. Or didn't expect us to come back. Stefano Asante slips in behind her. His eyes skate over us before he nods and heads to the back, slipping his headphones in.

Definitely should've skipped this one. Lorena Morelli jumps straight back into repeating the information she already gave us last time, and I can feel my eyes starting to glaze over. Dom looks a little sick when I look his way, and I can't hold in my snort. Luc leans in. "If you laugh, she starts again. *Don't.*"

All of us jerk, Dom snapping to full awareness as something smacks Luc straight in the center of his black shirt. He looks down incredulously at the splodge of white.

"Luciano." The old woman wipes off her hands of chalk and points at him. "Repeat what I just said."

His mouth opens, but nothing comes out. Dom snickers next to me.

"You. Corvo." I straighten when she points at me. The distracted, dizzy appearance is gone, replaced by a shrewd eye as she stares at me. "Repeat it."

"I... can't say that I was paying attention."

Lorena humphs. "And if you were being interviewed by the *polizia*? What then?"

A dull flush spreads across my face as she stares at us, waiting for a response that doesn't come.

"These are your final months," she says finally. "You've spent years learning the letter of the law, and how to circumvent it. There isn't much more I can teach you that would be useful at this point. But the mistake lies in thinking you know everything."

She turns, flopping down into the chair. "Your *mistake would* be in underestimating anyone. We do not have the luxury of being lazy. The *polizia* will drag out questioning for hours, repeating the same things over and over until your eyes glaze over. Until all you want to do is sleep. They will tie you up in knots, work you over and then trip you up on a technicality that puts you away for twenty to life."

She smirks. "Unless you fucking well *pay attention*. And I'm your great-aunt, Luciano Morelli. Not your damn third cousin. I changed your shitty diapers, you can at least remember the familial connection."

Luciano chokes, and I lean forward.

I *like* this woman.

"Now, then." She reaches up and cracks her neck, the sound making Dom shudder. "Someone get me a fucking strong coffee, black, three sugars, and I'll teach you some tricks they won't have covered in your *education*."

C*aterina*

We stagger out of Lorena's lesson a few hours later. Dom shakes his head in disbelief. "What just happened?"

"A verbal smackdown we needed." I flip through the pages of notes I took. Lorena is a fucking machine. I could have stayed there all day.

Luc pauses next to me, stretching his arms up and revealing a band of sleek, golden muscle. "At least she likes you. She seems to fucking hate me."

"Probably the shitty diapers." Dom's words are deadpan, and I choke back my laugh. But Luc turns to me, any mirth wiped away and replaced with a purely business expression. "I want to speak to you."

Scanning the empty corridor, I wave my hand. "Standing right here."

He glances at Domenico, and my lips press together. Dom looks between us with a frown. "I'll be down there."

We both watch him leave. "Talk, Luciano. I don't have the luxury of hanging around in deserted corridors at the moment."

"I know." His hazel eyes are dark as he faces me. He scans me up and down. "How are you doing?"

"I—what?"

His arms cross. "I'm asking if you're alright, Caterina," he says mildly. "No need to look at me like a slapped fish."

I snap my mouth closed, mortified. "I was *not*!"

"Honestly." He rolls his eyes. "Put a death sentence over her head and she doesn't bat an eye. Compare her to a fish and the world will end."

Frowning, I look past him to where Dom is leaning against the wall, his eyes scanning up and down. "Luc, I need to go. So can you just get on with it?"

He sighs, flicking a piece of invisible lint from the cuff of his shirt. "You have the use of the Morelli men for security, if you need them. None of them will try to complete the kiss. Tell your enforcer to link in with Nico and he'll co-ordinate."

Luc's enforcer. The words take a second to sink in, and I'm... blindsided. "Why would you do that?"

It's a generous offer. Incredibly so. It cuts down my list of possible opponents by a quarter. And with the additional men... I might have a chance of making it, at least until the end of the year when I walk through the gates for the last time.

I'm trying not to think about the fact that I might be living under the threat of *il bacio della morte* for *years*. And if not, it's because I'm already six feet under.

My stomach fizzes when I look back at Luc. There's a small smile on his face. "You don't know?"

Frowning, I tilt my head. "Did we sign an alliance when I wasn't looking?"

He smirks. "No alliance. But the offer is genuine. I have my own reasons for wanting you to stay alive, little crow."

When I hesitate, he goes to leave. "Wait. Luc... thank you."

He doesn't turn around. "No need to thank me, Caterina Corvo."

Dom slides past him, heading back towards me as I blink, rooted to the spot. "Cat? What happened?"

When I tell him, I'm not sure who looks more surprised.

Dom's face twists.

"Damn fucker was right," he mutters, and I jerk my head up.

"What?"

He shakes his head and checks his watch. "We need lunch. Come on."

He hasn't answered my question, but I leave it, too busy turning over the generous offer in my head. Searching for a trap.

There has to be something.

Caterina

I knew it was coming.

It was inevitable, really.

But even so, it still takes me by surprise.

The dining hall is full when we get there. Dom pauses, and I sweep past him, ignoring his grunted displeasure. I'm as well-prepared as I'm ever going to be, knives and guns in place, this time strapped over a pretty lace scarlet bodysuit that pushes my breasts *up* and *out*.

I may have taken the tiniest bit of pleasure in Dom's face when I walked out wearing it.

Right before he tried to march me back into the bedroom to '*get fucking dressed, right now*'.

Needless to say, I'm wearing the damn suit. So I'm a little smug as I yank the doors open and walk in. My heels are black tonight, matching the sleek leather pencil skirt. Not the most practical items, but these have a different purpose.

I pass the Asante table first, my Crows spreading out behind me. Men look up... and then down. The number of slack jaws on display is satisfyingly decent.

The Morellis, next. Nico catches my eye, nodding once. He and Dom have already spoken, and it appears that Luciano's offer is genuine, whatever his reasons. There are no angry looks, everyone glancing up and then quickly back to their business.

The V'Arezzos are a mixed bag. I get a few looks, some lascivious, some hate-filled. One particularly nasally little weasel coughs out an insult, puffing his chest up as he searches among his friends for approval.

He shrinks back when I pause, my eyes settling on him. "I'm sorry? I don't think I quite caught that."

He shakes his head, the tips of his ears turning pink, and his friends snicker.

As I turn away, I hear it again.

"*Whore.*"

A choked laugh is abruptly smothered. Up on the dais, Dante straightens, picking up on the tension at his table despite not being able to hear what we're saying.

My sigh is loud enough to draw more attention as I slide the knife out from the sheath under my arm, tonight on full display. I wasn't expecting to use it *quite* so soon. Especially on a sniveling little dickface like this.

"Once was a dick move. But twice is just fucking asking for it."

His mouth opens, but the knife is already flying. He topples over with a shocked grunt, the friends around him scattering as I glide over and yank the blade from the top of his shoulder. He whimpers.

"Feel free to try and insult me again some time." I tap his cheek with the blade, and I think he might piss himself. "Properly, this time. Maybe when your balls have dropped."

No. Scratch that. He has pissed himself.

One of the girls laughs as I move out of the danger zone, her cheeks coloring when I catch her eye. She grins, and I wonder if Dante knows that he's got an asshole like this one in his ranks. I sense from her reaction that she's not displeased with the show.

I'm distracted, so much so that I'm a second too late in responding when Dom roars my name. The Crows are still on the walkway, too far away to be of any help as I twist around to look for the danger.

It's the twist that saves my life. The knife slices my neck as I stagger back, a thin, burning line across my skin as the Crows throw themselves on top of the Fusco asshole who thought he could take me out with my *own fucking trick*.

"Cat." Dom is there, his hands gently inspecting my neck. "Jesus Christ. Pay fucking attention."

"Don't shout at me when I have a stab wound," I snap back, and he just scowls, his finger prodding at it until I hiss, pushing his hands away.

"That's not a stab wound. It's cut, but I don't think it'll scar. You just took ten years off my fucking life!"

"It was a lucky break. Let him go." My voice rises as I call out, and Vincent looks over, panting as he and Tony struggle to contain the man.

"Uh – not sure that's a good idea, Cat."

My would-be murderer wrenches himself free, drawing himself up to face me. His face twists into a sneer. "Gonna set your dogs on me, bitch?"

Fucking *hell*. Enough with the misogynistic insults, already. No wonder the Cosa Nostra is decades behind the rest of the world when it comes to female empowerment.

"I'm not going to punish you for being a decent shot," I say coldly. "Although the insults coming from this room make me a little concerned for the future of the English language."

I glance around him. The Fuscos watch me with anger, Rosa Fusco front and center.

"The next person to throw a knife at me gets it back in their throat."

Now thoroughly pissed off because I can feel blood dripping down and staining my bodysuit, I spin on my heel and make for my chair. All the heirs are there, watching me with varying expressions. Naturally, Stefano is stoic and still. Luc's face is curved in amusement, his eyes tracking the blood dripping as he pulls out the middle seat between him and Dante and I throw myself into it with a huff.

Dante looks ready to fight someone – possibly me, since I just stabbed one of his precious V'Arezzos. Giovanni looks straight ahead, not deigning to look in my direction, but there's a slight curve to his mouth as he nods to his man in clear approval.

"You know he missed, right?" I can't help but throw down the table. "Didn't have you pegged for one of those who thinks *all* the minions deserve an A for effort no matter how shit they are, Fusco."

He turns to me with a smirk, raising his glass. "He drew first blood. The hunt has started, Caterina. I look forward to seeing how long you last."

"I'm not surprised," I say. My lips curl into a sympathetic smile, and he raises an eyebrow questioningly. "Because I heard *you* don't last very long at all."

It's childish as fuck, but it makes me feel better anyway. The table is suddenly full of coughs. Even Stefano looks like he might crack a smile when I glance behind me.

Only Gio looks unamused. He turns away. "Enjoy the jokes while you can."

It turns out nearly getting my neck cut makes me hungry as hell. I demolish the giant plate of seafood pasta Dom hands me in a few minutes. He shakes his head when I catch his eye and try to point unobtrusively towards the buffet for a second helping.

It's definitely a punishment for the bodysuit.

Slumping, I blink as another helping slides onto my plate. "You know, Morelli, people are going to start talking if you keep doing nice things for me."

"Eat your pasta." His voice is moody, and when I glance up, his eyes are still pinned to my neck. "And then go and get that looked at."

Assessing the pasta and ignoring Dom's irritated face, I decide that it's highly unlikely Luc would poison himself just to get to me and start working my way through. It takes me a few minutes to come up for air. "It's not as bad as it looks."

"It looks fucking horrendous." His knuckles are white as they wrap around the arm of his chair. "Don't be a fool, little crow. You get too confident, and someone *will* catch you. You're not invincible."

"You say that like you'd miss me if I was gone."

The words slip out, teasing in a way I'd normally reserve for Domenico, and I'm too late to yank them back. Frowning, I stare into my empty plate.

For Dom, yes, but not for Luciano Morelli. Our discussions are normally a mixture of veiled threats and pointed jibes.

When we were fourteen, he spent an entire year editing photos of me with spots all over my face and sending them to my phone. All because I had *one* particularly gross spot on my chin, and I turned up at a Cosa Nostra social with a little too much concealer on it. He laughed himself hoarse. I made my father pay for a specialist skin treatment.

When we were sixteen... well. We don't talk about that particular moment of insanity. Ever.

But this is not what we do.

Enough time passes that I deem it safe enough to look up. But it's a mistake.

Because when I do, he's right there, those too damn pretty hazel eyes fixed to my face.

"Maybe I would miss you," he says softly. "Because this world would be a fucking miserable place without you in it, little crow."

It might be the single nicest thing he's ever said to me. And my fucking stomach *flips*.

Shit.

Shit.

I stand up in a fluster, pulling myself together just enough to watch for any more flying knives as I almost run from the hall. Dom and my entourage of bodyguards follow me, Dom demanding to know what the matter is as I fend him off with weak excuses about my neck hurting.

He doesn't buy it. I know he doesn't. But neither of us say anything as he patches up the cut, cleaning it and confirming it doesn't need stitches before I tell him I need space. Ignoring the hurt in his eyes as he leaves, taking up a post outside and telling me to lock the doors.

Once I'm locked in, I crawl into bed, tugging the covers over my head. Breathing deeply, I try to work out exactly why the *fuck* I seem to be having feelings for three men at the same time.

None of whom are an appropriate choice.

All of whom seem to be looking in my direction.

I'm no good at this. Put a gun in my hand and point me at a target? I'll hit it every time. Knives? Fucking *yes*. The possibility of death? I'll face it with a smile on my face and I'll take as many of my fucking enemies down as I can with me.

But men? That's a minefield I've never been particularly good at navigating.

Pulling out my phone, I send Amie a message to ask if she's still awake, but the phone remains dark in my hand.

This is something I need my one and only female friend to help with.

I will also need wine.

Lots of wine.

Caterina

I keep my head down in training the next morning.

My stomach churns, demanding food, but I shove it down and focus on running. I skipped breakfast, too exhausted from a sleepless night to risk a showdown I might not win in my current, sleep-deprived condition.

A shame that I can't actually run away from my problems, but I'll give it a damn good go. I steadfastly ignore the looks slanted my way from both Dante and Luciano. Stefano doesn't even look up when I snag the treadmill next to his, and for once I revel in his silence.

At least Dom's not here, although I have no doubts he'll be waiting by the door when I leave.

Even Vito leaves me alone this morning, choosing to bellow insults at Dante and Luc instead as they run through a weights routine.

I check my phone again, but there's nothing. No reply from Amie, and nothing from my father. I've tried to call several times this morning, each one sent to voicemail until I finally gave up. My stomach churns again, another headache forming behind my eyes.

He's ignoring me. Even Aldo isn't picking up my calls, and the thought of what might be happening at home makes the pain even worse.

Slowing the machine, I wait for it to stop before I sag, resting my head on the railing. A full bottle of water slides into my view, and I glance over to where Stefano is packing his stuff away. "Thanks."

Breaking the seal, I swig it down gratefully, chasing the nausea away until my stomach feels uncomfortably full.

It could be nothing. My father is a busy man, after all.

But he always made time for you before, the bitchy little voice in my head whispers.

Before I disappointed him. Before he started raising his *concerns*.

Dom slips inside as I pack my own shit up, and I wait until the room is clear. "I need you to go home and check on things."

I already know he's going to argue. Sinking down onto a bench, I roll the water across my forehead, chasing the ache away.

"I'm not leaving you."

His tone is non-negotiable, but I'm not budging.

"I'm not asking. I'm *telling* you, Domenico. Vincent can take over for a day or two. We can put extra people on the rota. The Morellis will help. But I want you there. Feel things out."

"Cat." He sounds torn.

"Something is wrong." I don't look at him. "Something's going on, Dom, and I can't focus until I know. I have to know, and there is nobody else. You know there's not. *Please*."

He sinks down next to me. "Two days. Two days, and I'll be back, Cat. Tell me you can last two damn days."

I blow out a breath. "I can last two days."

Maybe.

"I mean it." He looks at me, really looks at me. Like he's examining my soul.

Like he might never see me again.

"Don't look at me like that," I mumble.

"Like what?"

Like I mean something.

"Like you're saying goodbye," I say instead. "Have faith in me, Dom."

His hand slides across my cheek, cupping it and tilting it towards him.

"I will always have faith in you, Caterina Corvo. You wouldn't be my endgame if I didn't."

I have to close my eyes. I don't know what to do with the look in his face, how to respond to the burning in his eyes. But my breath catches as soft lips press against mine. He tastes like cherries, like the gum he has a sneaky preference for that he thinks I don't know about.

Something uniquely Domenico.

Familiar and new at the same time.

"Don't fucking die," he whispers against my mouth. "And lock your doors."

When I open my eyes again, he's gone.

Dramatic, overprotective bastard.

But my fingers still reach up to touch my lips anyway.

Caterina

In a move that would probably make Dom drop dead from shock, I opt to lie low for the next few days. I eat my meals in the apartment, skip training, work from the little office in the back instead of heading to the building set aside for our use.

I don't admit that I miss my enforcer. That it feels like my left arm is missing without him here.

Two men try to break in on the first night Dom is gone. Tony and Vincent call me apologetically out of bed, and I don't tell them that I wasn't sleeping anyway.

These two have no knives on them. Just rope.

I strip them myself and send them back to Giovanni, hog-tied and red-faced, a note around their necks.

I believe these belong to you.

Any further lost property will be disposed of.

Nobody tries on the second night, but that could be because I already have an uninvited visitor.

I'm making coffee when the telltale creak of movement sounds outside. It takes me a moment to check the cameras, to see the familiar silhouette, and for anger to rise in my stomach.

Dante gives me a slow smile when I rip the door open. "What the fuck are you doing here, Dante?"

He stretches his arms above his head. "Guard duty. All agreed with your own personal guard dog, *tentazione*. I wouldn't mind a coffee if there's one going."

The slamming of the door in his face is the only answer I give, my fingers already flying as I type out a message to Dom.

Are you and Dante working together?

The dots bubble up, and then disappear again. My feet tread a path past the front door and back again, until the phone vibrates in my hand.

We have a mutual interest. Behave.

I nearly choke on my own tongue.

You hate each other.

Well, maybe we like you more. Why aren't you sleeping?

I check the time, swearing when I realize it's after two.

I woke up because he was making so much noise with his elephant feet.

His response comes a second later.

Liar.

I shouldn't be surprised when the door knocks a minute later. Dante looks irritated when I pull it open. "I do not have elephant feet."

"Good to know," I deadpan. "I'm going to sleep now."

He taps his phone. "I know. I have strict instructions."

Ignoring the sarcasm, I seize the phone and stare down at the message. My traitorous enforcer has indeed sent him a message.

She's not sleeping again. Make her.

And above that—

"Memes." My voice is disbelieving.

Dante yanks the phone away from me, and a hint of color flares high on his chiseled cheekbones. "Do you always scroll through people's private messages?"

I squint at him. "You and Dom are meme buddies. *Muddies*."

They might be visual interpretations of all the ways they'd like to see each other die, but it's almost... sweet.

"What the fuck is—you know what? Doesn't matter. Bed. Now."

He grabs my wrist, not so gently, and starts tugging me towards the bedroom.

"Woah, Tarzan," I mutter. "Could at least take me to dinner first."

Dante turns to me, confusion drawing his eyebrows down low. "Are you drunk?"

I click my tongue. "High on life, I'm afraid. Also, let go of my wrist, or I will snap it."

"That's better." He sounds relieved as he pulls me through the bedroom door and loosens his grip. "Now get into bed."

He points at the covers like he actually expects me to get in. The smirk spreads across my face as I lean against the door. "I'm not tired."

He crosses his arms. "The purple smudges under your eyes suggest otherwise. They seem to have grown to the size of a small country."

I examine my nails. "Thank you for that completely unwarranted and borderline rude offering. Most people bring a *gift* when they turn up to somebody's home unannounced. Feel free to leave now."

When I look up, he's only a few inches away from me. "Who says I don't have a gift for you?"

Blinking, I look around me obviously. "If you do that thing where you announce that you're the gift, I will never find you attractive again. Just to say."

The half smile on his face grows. "So you *do* still find me attractive. Good to know."

I feel like I'm losing control of this conversation. The lack of sleep is hitting me hard. Pushing my tongue into the side of my mouth, I debate how to respond.

Dante moves closer still, until he's caging me against the door. His voice drops to a whisper as he leans in. "Why don't you let me take that edge off for you, *tentazione*? I hear that several back-to-back orgasms work wonders for a good night's sleep."

I can't say I'm not tempted. But my heart still stings from the memory of his vicious words. The way he called me a whore with his scent still clinging to my skin.

"I don't fuck men who call me a slut one day and then expect me to crawl into bed with them the next. If you want to play the protector, Dante, be my guest. But you have no right to *me*. And if you want to know who's responsible for that, go and look in the fucking mirror."

He pulls away from me like I've physically landed a blow, and I duck out from under his arm, moving to stand by the door.

He twists to look at me, and for the first time, he looks... uncertain.

"I didn't mean it," he breathes. "Surely you know that."

I wrap my arms around me. "But you still said it. So the question is, do *you* know that?"

He glowers at me. "Of course I do. I was angry, and I took it out on you, you stubborn *principessa*. You *infuriate* me."

"Ah," I say wearily. "Well, that's fine then. Glad to know that your anger issues are my fucking fault, Dante. All is forgiven. Happy to be your verbal punching bag anytime."

He groans then, rubbing his hands down his face before he responds. "I'm fucking this up, but I'm trying to apologise, Cat. I *am* sorry. So fucking sorry I said that. Of course it's not true."

Pursing my lips, I glance out to the living room. "Even if it was, you don't get to judge me for what I do with my own body. If I want to fuck my way through half the campus, I damn well will."

Red flag to a bull. He takes a step closer, brows dipping. "You damn well will *not*."

God save me from the possessive assholes around me. "I'm not having this discussion with you. Consider me sufficiently exhausted from your presence. Leave. Now."

"Fine," he snaps, stalking past me. "I'll be outside if you need me."

He slams my front door behind him, so hard the walls rattle.

"*Cretino*," I hiss, slamming my bedroom door even though he can't see it. It still makes me feel better. "*Cazzone*."

Fucking *men*.

Domenico

Bea puts another plate of food down in front of me, and I have to protest, my stomach groaning. "I can't possibly eat anymore, *sorella*. You've fed me enough to last the rest of the month."

She swats the back of my head in response as she walks away, and Pepe laughs. My sister's husband is a good man, low enough in the hierarchy to escape most of the political bullshit that comes with it. Something my sister is grateful for. "I would finish your plate, Dom. She's making up for the time since we last saw you."

Guilt at the reproof in his words has me digging in. I haven't been home for a while, too wrapped up in Caterina and the constant fucking headache of trying to keep her safe. Before that, I had no choice, trying to keep the Crows afloat while she was gone.

It's been... months, actually.

A mournful wail rises up from the other room, and Pepe slips from his seat with an apologetic murmur. I wait until he reappears, cradling the baby in his arms. Alessia makes another frustrated noise, and he laughs as he props her up on the table. She kicks her feet out as he curves one arm around her protectively and continues eating with the other. "She's growing up too fast."

"She's sitting up now?" I ask, watching the little girl wave her fists. She eyes me uncertainly, and I have to smile.

"She is. And she crawls, when she has a mind to," my sister answers. She scoops Alessia up, cooing to her, and the baby laughs joyfully. "Don't you, *tesoro mia*? Perhaps your Uncle Domenico would like to hold you while I eat. Since he's so *full*."

I open my mouth, but my sister expertly wrangles Alessia into my arms, sitting down beside me with a wink and a reassuring pat to my arm. "She doesn't bite."

I wouldn't be so sure. The little girl settles against my chest, a soft, warm, curly-haired bundle in her flannel dress. A bright ring of green stands out vividly around her hazel irises as she stares at me. Experimentally, I hold out my finger and she follows the movement, grabbing for it and gripping on. A happy little gurgle comes from her chest, and she smiles up at me, wide and gummy.

So innocent, it makes my chest hurt. She feels out of place in my arms, like I might accidentally hurt her, so I stay still, letting her play with my hand as she pushes my fingers apart and closes them again, over and over.

"That's one hell of a grip you've got there, *piccolo*. Just like your mother."

Bea laughs, leaning over and running her finger over Alessia's cheek. "She will be a heartbreaker, this one. So, am I allowed to ask why you've deigned to visit us lowly mortals?"

My cheeks redden. "Bea."

"Bah." She waves her hand carelessly. "I know, I know. Busy men and their busy lives. The Cosa Nostra is not forgiving with its needs. Pepe barely gets home in time to eat these days."

My eyes move to my brother-in-law. He's watching his wife, but he shakes his head the tiniest amount. So I don't enquire, instead teasing the sister who raised me after our parents died when I was ten. Alessia's grip slowly slackens on my finger, her eyes sliding closed as her cheek rests against my heart.

I wonder if she can hear it.

"Here," Bea whispers. Carefully, she lifts the little girl into her arms, leaving a cold space behind. "I'll take her to bed, leave you to talk."

Her hand brushes Pepe's face and he presses a kiss to her palm, sitting back as the door closes softly. "This is not a good time, Domenico."

"I'm here for information." My hands tap on the table. "There is a disconnect between the campus and the family. What's happening?"

Pepe shrugs, but his eyes crease in concern. "You know I'm not close enough to know everything. But... Matteo is everywhere, Dom. He used to be in the background, but Joseph is giving him more and more work."

"Wet work?" I ask, and he scowls.

"What happened to the Fusco girl... it didn't land well. Most of his senior men had reservations. It's caused a lot of talk. I don't think it's wet work. More that he's distracting him with other things. He's put him in charge of the protection scheme."

My hands stop tapping. "That's... insane. He's the last person who should be involved in that. He's not stable enough."

The Corvos have a tight grip on the New York area. The community trusts us. They trust us to protect them, and in exchange, we maintain a healthy stream of income. Income that gets laundered through the university, or through some of our other businesses.

Pepe leans forward. "He's raised prices twice in the last few weeks. And the punishment for refusal is not one any of us would want to face. He's using it as an excuse to torture people, Dom, and Joseph is *letting* him."

Shit. "Any mention of Caterina?"

My hackles go up when he hesitates. "Matteo... Matteo is spreading rumors. That she's weak. That she's being managed by the other heirs. That the Fuscos are more confident because she is failing, Dom. Cat has allies here, but they're getting quieter by the day. Nobody wants to draw Matteo's attention."

This... this is a fucking takeover attempt. "What's Joseph saying?"

He sighs. "Matteo has his ear, and he is dripping poison constantly. What happened... it has not helped her, Domenico. Word has not spread, but Joseph's opinion is the only one that matters. Joseph is concerned that she is not up to the job, and he will not consider her if he feels that the power he has gathered is at risk. He would replace her with Matteo. He has cut her off to force her to step up, or he will make her step down."

It feels like someone has punched me directly in the solar plexus. "Matteo is not his true heir. He's not even a close blood relation. What is he, a second cousin?"

And Joseph has always been fanatical about bloodlines.

Pepe looks grim. "There is another rumor. That Joseph may try for a new heir. A male, this time. He wouldn't care if Matteo was only a temporary fix. He's still a fit man. Plenty of time before someone else needs to take over. That truly is a rumor, though. Matteo may even be spreading it himself, for all I know. There may be nothing to it, but I figured you should know."

"Thank you, Pepe. How are things here?"

He shakes his head. "I keep my head down and do my job, Dom. Nobody has looked at us twice. But Bea and I are ready, if the wind changes. You know where our loyalty stands."

My throat feels tight as I stand, reaching out to grip his hand. "I do. And I am grateful, Pepe."

More grateful than I can put words to. As I'm pulling on my jacket, a shadow appears in the doorway. Bea is frowning.

"You're leaving already?"

I glance back at her. "I can't stay, Bea. I have to make a few stops before I can head back. Things are difficult at the moment."

She sighs, but she reaches forward to wrap her arms around my waist. She feels tiny in my grip, so different from how it used to be.

"It's always difficult. When did you get so damn tall?" Her familiar complaint makes me grin, and I squeeze her tighter. "Take care of yourself, you hear?"

"I will." She stands back. "And I'll take care of them too."

I know that. My sister will fight to her last breath for her family.

"Some things go without saying, *sorella*."

CATERINA

When I scan the brightly lit screen in front of me, my eyebrows lift.

I run the checks again.

And again.

Every time, I get the same result.

It's not exactly what I need. Not yet, anyway.

But it's getting there.

A knock on the office door jerks me out of my concentration, and I sit up as Vincent sticks his head around the door. "Sorry to disturb you, Cat. You're running late for training. Figured you'd want to know."

My eyes fly to the clock above the wall. "Thanks, Vincent. I'll meet you outside."

With a nod, he softly closes the door behind him. He works differently to Dom – quiet and respectful, as opposed to domineering and argumentative as hell.

Nice, but not what I need.

As we walk over to the training center, Vincent stays a half-step behind me. I can feel his eyes, scanning everywhere, behind and in front. The others with him do the same.

Not wanting to distract him, I stay silent, my eyes flicking towards the gaps between buildings. But no monsters jump out at us today, although my shoulders are tight with tension as Vincent escorts me into the center, hesitating at the door to the changing rooms. "You want me in there with you?"

I shake my head. "Outside. I'll be done in an hour."

When I walk in, Dante and Stefano are already there, although there's no sign of Luciano.

And so is Giovanni.

Surprised, I pause. He sees me in the mirror and sits up from the bench. "Caterina. Still alive, I see."

"Easily done when you're dealing with incompetence, Fusco."

Vito heads our way, his head darting between us. "Keep it out of my session. Cleaning blood from the floor in here is a fucker."

There's more than one old, rusty-looking stain on the floor to lend truth to his irritated words.

Ignoring Gio, I head over to the bars and start stretching. I've been slacking lately, the tightness of my muscles telling me exactly how out of shape I am compared to how I used to be. Taking up a spot on the floor, I move into sit-ups, forcing myself to push harder and harder until I can feel the sweat trickling down my back. Once I've completed the third set of thirty, I let myself collapse back to the floor, my hands moving to cover my aching abdomen.

Definitely out of shape.

Vito shouts something that sounds vaguely insulting in my direction, and I stick my finger in the air in response. The deep laugh that sounds is much closer than Vito's voice, and my eyes snap open as a shadow falls across my face, blocking out the bright light from the strips overhead. "Ever heard of personal space, Morelli?"

Luc clicks his tongue, holding out his hand. His eyebrow raises in a silent challenge, and I grab it with a huff, letting him pull me up. He's not dressed for a workout, decked out in his usual smart black shirt and trousers. "You've been avoiding me, Caterina."

"Believe it or not, my whole world doesn't actually revolve around you." Dropping his hand, I duck around him, but he only turns and follows me to the weights section.

He frowns as I load up. "Little light for you, isn't it?"

"Did I ask you to comment on my workout routine?" I snap. "What do you want? You're obviously not here to work out."

He watches me for a moment, before he lifts the case in his left hand. "I came to show you my latest acquisitions, actually. Thought you might... appreciate them."

I glance around the room, noting the eyes on us. "Here?"

He shrugs. "As good a place as any. The dining hall is proving a little chaotic these days. And this is a space for weapons, after all."

He hefts the case, unlatching the brass hinges and flipping it open as I sit up. His eyes don't move from my face, his lips lifting at the corners as I stand, my attention well and truly caught.

The twin daggers look almost ceremonial at first glance. Perfectly tapered, thin bronze shaped like tridents, the middle part longer to form the blade. The handles, a silky-looking navy with gold threading built in for grip, glitter in the overhead light.

My breath catches. They're the most beautiful fucking weapons I've ever seen. I've been searching for daggers like these for *years.*

Luciano pushes the lid down. "You like them?"

Forcing my gaze away, I purse my lips. "Maybe. Where'd you get them?"

They look custom. Unique.

I have to force the want from my face. The need. And damn him, but Luc doesn't miss it. Those damn angelic lips twist up into a knowing grin.

"What will you give me for these pretty knives, Caterina?"

His voice is low, seductive. A threat. And as I glance around, I notice all eyes on us. Dante has stopped, frowning as he stares over. Giovanni's expressionless, but he watches anyway. Even Stefano's eyes are drifting in our direction.

I take a step closer to Luciano. He tilts his head as I lean in, his breathing shifting to something deeper.

"Give me the stabby things, Morelli," I murmur. My nail traces a line down his shirt, scraping the front of his trousers where none of the others can see, and I have the satisfaction of watching his pupils dilate as he shifts. "And maybe I won't try them out on you."

These men play their games, but they forget that I can play too.

My hand cups him, just in case he missed my fucking obvious warning.

I *want* those fucking knives.

"Consider them yours, then, little crow," Luc murmurs. My eyes flick up to his as his cock hardens under my hand. "I'm sure I'll be able to get another set."

I highly doubt it, but I offer him a sunny smile, my hand dropping from his trousers. "Why, thank you, Luciano. Very generous of you."

He holds out the case for me to take, and I wrap my arms around it protectively as I head for the door. As I pull it open, Giovanni's voice rings out.

"Picking sides, Morelli?"

But it's Luciano Morelli's drawled response that makes me pause. I turn to look over my shoulder, meeting his gaze, my new knives held tightly to my chest.

"Some of us chose a side a long time ago, Fusco."

It's only later, as I'm in the safety of the apartment examining my stolen present, running my finger reverently down the sleek handles, that I see the edge of letters etched into the base of the bronze. I flip them both over to look.

CC.

He already had my initials engraved into them.

Caterina

The car engine rumbles beneath me as I shift in my seat. Danny's eyes flit up, meeting mine in the mirror. "Any word from Domenico?"

I shake my head. I'm expecting him back this evening, but I won't be there to greet him.

No. Thanks to a brief text from my father with today's date and a time, I'm on my way to a Cosa Nostra meeting without my enforcer by my side. Normally arranged weeks in advance, tonight I had just a few hours to prepare.

And I don't feel particularly well-prepared at all.

This feels like a test. Or maybe a trap.

Grimacing, I pull out my phone. I'm tempted to ask Dante, to find out when he knew this would be happening, but I don't want to let on that I didn't know.

Nothing from Domenico, and still no response from Amie. I haven't seen her, thanks to my absence from the dining hall, and she's not responding to any of my messages.

It's not something I can think about now, though.

"Coming up to the gates," Danny calls. Straightening, I glance out of the window. The house rises up in the darkness, a large colonial mansion surrounded by acres of land. Used for the sole purpose of Cosa Nostra meetings, it never fails to look less than welcoming, despite the pretty exterior.

I take a minute to check my appearance in the small mirror I keep in the car for this exact reason. Thanks to the lack of notice, I didn't have time to straighten my chaotic hair, so I scraped it back into a low bun at the base of my neck. My eyes are dark, dusky rose eyeshadow lined with kohl to make them stand out. A hint of color sits on my cheeks, my lips deepened to dark red.

Appearances are everything, after all. Especially to the men that make up the heads of the Cosa Nostra.

Danny pulls up to the entrance, exiting and coming around to open the door. Mindful of eyes watching, I ignore his outstretched hand, vivid red heels clicking on the paved driveway as I slide out. Straightening my fitted blazer, I sweep past Danny and make my way up the steps.

A butler opens the door, one of the skeleton staff we keep on hand at all times. Although used by the Cosa Nostra, this technically belongs to my father in his role as *capo dei capi*.

The man bows. "Miss Corvo."

"Alvaro." I survey the candlelit entrance. "The usual place, I assume?"

At his confirmation, I head down the hallway. Sconces of candlelight flicker against the deep red walls, highlighting the expensive artwork on display.

All of it is useful. There is a huge amount of money to be made through the art world. If an anonymous buyer purchases a painting for more than it's worth, nobody truly bats an eyelid. Especially the authorities.

And if drugs are part of the deal, slipped in alongside the painting as part of the overall cost, well, nobody will know. The value of art is so subjective, after all.

Voices, the clinking of glasses and low laughter filter out from an open door ahead of me. The men that have accompanied the dons to tonight's meeting are all gathered inside. When I glance through, I spot Leo standing in the corner. He feels my eyes on him and looks up, baring his teeth.

Aldo, my father's enforcer is there too, buffeted from Leo by a handful of others, and he nods briefly at me before turning away.

Not a good sign.

As I reach the closed door to the meeting room, I don't stop. Instead, I throw it open and walk through.

The nine men inside turn to face me.

Luciano stands behind his father, Paul Morelli. One of the oldest here, gray-haired with lines of grief and laughter carved into his aging face. He used to slip me sweets when I was little, until I grew old enough to understand that taking any sort of edible from a rival family was a dangerous game.

Dante's arms are folded as he watches me from behind Frank V'Arezza. His father leans back in his chair, his eyes scanning the rest of the room as he turns away from me.

Stefano stands stiffly behind Salvatore Asante. They look as different as night and day. While Stefano is thickly built, heavily muscled with his shaved head and dark eyes, Salvatore is sleeker. His blonde hair is slicked back from his face, eyes of pale blue landing on me with a delighted smile. He's not an ugly man, at least on the outside.

He gives me the fucking creeps.

My eyes dance over my own father, taking in the stiffness of his jawline, before they land on Carlo Fusco. Just a glimpse is enough to tell me that Carlo is a broken man. The strong, still-handsome don has all but disappeared. He slumps in his seat, skin pale, barely paying attention to his surroundings. But Gio's lip curls as he meets my eye, daring me to look.

To see the damage we have caused.

"Caterina." My father stands. "Welcome."

My smile is a little sultry, a little cruel. Carefully crafted. "Thank you, papa."

Salvatore Asante practically licks his lips, his eyes on my body as I move past him to take up my post, and I hold back my visible distaste with a concerted effort. Now is not the time to piss off my father by antagonizing his biggest ally.

And the tension is high enough. Carlo doesn't seem aware of much at all as he blinks, his gaze hazy. But Giovanni's fury at standing in the same room as the man who ordered his sister's death is clear, his anger hovering over us like a storm.

My father simply settles back in his chair, ignoring him altogether, and it only seems to make the storm more turbulent. "Now that everyone is present, we can begin. Salvatore, start us off."

I steel myself to listen. The Asantes specialize in the movement of cargo.

Drugs, weapons. Black market goods.

Anything that needs moving, they'll move, for the right price.

Including women.

It's never been publicly acknowledged, even in these meetings, but having met Salvatore Asante, it's not hard to believe.

He grumbles for twenty minutes about border controls and insurance, before Frank V'Arezzo takes over. His update is a brief and concise overview, focused on the gambling businesses they oversee from their headquarters in Nevada.

Giving as little information as possible, but not too little to be accused of holding back. Dante notices me watching, but he doesn't give anything away as his father speaks.

There is no Dante and Caterina here. Only the V'Arezzo and Corvo heirs, here to observe, ready to take up our own seats one day.

Exactly what I tried to tell him before. Maybe he understands now, as we look at each other from across the table.

Paul Morelli's update is a little more detailed. The Morellis don't have a set specialism, although their involvement in the art world is extensive. He glances up at Luciano when he pauses, and to my surprise, Luc steps forward, clearing his throat.

Everyone shifts as he continues his father's update, Paul watching him closely. As he steps back, my father lifts his hand.

"Are we to expect a succession soon?" he asks directly, and Paul tilts his shoulders with a sly smile.

"I'm not dead yet." A few titters around the table. "But I prefer to be prepared."

My father assesses Luciano with more focus, and his eyes narrow as he taps his hand on the wood in front of us. Luc keeps his gaze straight ahead. "Interesting."

My father considers him for a few more movements, and then his eyes move. "Fusco. Still alive over there?"

Giovanni jerks, and I bite the inside of my cheek, hard, at the cold cruelty in my father's voice.

Gio glances down at his father, his jaw tightening. Carlo Fusco drags his eyes up, slowly. He opens his mouth, and then closes it again.

His son steps forward, his mouth set in a hard line. "I have the update."

"You haven't been given permission to speak, boy." My father's voice sounds like a whip, cutting through the quiet. "Until you are, I suggest you close your mouth."

He leans back, perfectly at ease. His chair squeaks. "We all know what happens to those who can't follow orders."

Gio's whole body locks up. His fists clench.

Don't, I send him silently. *Don't do it.*

But he's not looking at me. No, his eyes are locked onto my father. "Yes," he spits. "Their daughters end up raped and butchered, their body pieces scattered across our *fucking* lawn."

"Enough."

The word doesn't come from my father. No, that's *my* fucking mouth opening, everyone turning to me with mixed expressions. Luciano wipes away his horrified look, but Dante isn't so quick.

"*Cat*," he hisses.

My father, though, his body stills. Dante shuts up, fast, but my father still glances between us before he turns to me. "Caterina. Speak."

The warning, the cold radiating from my name, is enough to tell me that I am in the *shit*. Even Gio turns his eyes to me. Quickly, I wave my hand, adopting an expression just as icy as my father's voice.

"Clearly, Fusco is incapacitated." My voice is steady, expressionless. "I, for one, have commitments this evening that cannot wait. Let the heir speak, or we'll all be here until midnight waiting around."

I can barely breathe as my father watches me closely. Finally, he nods slowly, turning to Gio. "Consider this your one and only reprieve, Fusco. Interesting that it came from my daughter, when you have placed *il bacio della morte* upon her head."

I wonder who told him. It certainly wasn't me, since he's not answering my calls. To his credit, Giovanni doesn't flinch, staring down my father as he delivers the Fusco report in clipped tones. It explains why he's been absent most of the time from our joint tutoring sessions. Picking up the workload. Taking on the mantle sooner than he should have to.

The circles under his eyes are darker than mine.

When my father eventually dismisses us, Gio is the first to leave, taking his father's arm and almost lifting him from his seat. It's painful to watch, and I have to look away.

It's when my eyes fall to the floor that I feel it.

Fingers trail up the inside of my leg, brushing against my inner thigh. Spreading out.

Moving higher in small circles. Harder. More demanding.

Gripping.

My back snaps ramrod straight, black spots dancing in front of my vision.

A wave of frost runs down my spine as I breathe in. Breathe out. My hands start to shake. When I glance at my father, he's absorbed in watching Gio.

Everyone is watching Gio.

My eyes slide to the seat next to me. Salvatore Asante has his eyes on the doorway, but his hand... his hand is gripping the inside of my thigh, a whisper away from my underwear.

Heat chases down the frost, dousing it in steam and leaving flickering flame in its wake. I slam my legs together, as hard as I can, and Salvatore's grip loosens. I swallow a choked gasp as my skin is twisted, gripped hard in long fingers, nails digging in.

Stefano glances back at me as the smallest, pained noise escapes my lips.

His eyes drop down. Further.

Just in time to catch the hand being pulled away.

His lips part, and he stares down at his father. A look of disgust crosses his face. I feel his eyes on my face, but I'm not looking at him.

Salvatore has a smile on his face as he settles his hands back onto the table, leaving aching, bruised skin behind. I blink rapidly, vomit rising up my throat.

A punishment, maybe. For speaking up.

For existing at all.

A reminder of my *place*.

Breathing in, I take my time pushing the oxygen out, making sure my voice won't shake when I speak. My fingers slip beneath the sleeve of my blazer.

"Salvatore."

People turn at my snapped tone. My father turns.

And Salvatore Asante *screams* as my blade slams into his hand, deep enough that it goes straight through and into the table, deep enough to part flesh and sever tendons. Stefano jumps back as curses ring through the room. Shouts.

But I ignore them, drawing myself up as Salvatore moans in shock, staring at his ravaged hand.

"If you *ever*." My voice doesn't shake. I refuse to let it, refuse to let him have the satisfaction of even the tiniest part of the fear clogging my throat, clawing at my stomach. "*Ever*, try to touch me in that way again. If I ever see you touching another woman in that way, I will cut off your fucking hand. *Be grateful you still have it.*"

I have to leave.

Before they see my body shaking.

Before the aching in my throat can turn into the tears burning the back of my eyes.

So I sweep out, past a gaping Giovanni and the ruined, ravaged shell of Carlo Fusco.

And I don't look back, leaving my blade in his flesh.

As a reminder not to touch what doesn't fucking belong to him.

Dante

Someone is roaring.

But as Cat leaves, her face pale and her head high, I realize the rest of the room is silent. Silent, apart from the gasping of Salvatore Asante.

The roaring is me. The sound building inside my head.

I take a step forward, and a hand wraps around my arm, holding tightly. A voice hisses in my ear. "You won't help her by interfering, V'Arezzo."

Luciano's voice is glacial, but it cuts through the noise. My father glances back at me, a small shake of his head.

Damn them. Damn them both to fucking hell for being right.

I want to kill him. Tear the fucking head off his body, finish the job that Cat started and take off his fucking hands myself.

He fucking *touched* her.

My heart pounds inside my chest, the pumping sound harsh in my ears as Joseph Corvo stands, his eyes sweeping over the fucking filth whining as he tries to pull his hand free. Even Stefano looks repulsed as he watches him.

Caterina's father leans forward and rips out the dagger. As Salvatore howls, Joseph turns the blade over in his hands, his expression considering.

Bland.

Then he offers him the fucking handle. "I trust the matter is concluded?"

Cunt.

I'm glad Cat isn't here as Salvatore grits his teeth, taking the blade with his other hand. "It is."

"Good." Joseph flicks his eyes over us all. And then he walks out.

Just walks out, like he doesn't give a flying fuck that his daughter was just assaulted by his so-called friend. The bile rises again in my throat at the casual dismissal.

Gio disappears with his father, and Luc gives me a final look before following Paul Morelli out of the room. My own father returns to my side. "Let's go."

Nodding slowly, I begin to follow him out, and then pause.

Turning, I walk back to where Salvatore is tugging off his tie and wrapping it around his bleeding hand. As he starts to turn around, my hand shoots out.

The sound as his face meets the heavy table in front is satisfying as fuck, even as my father groans. Asante slumps to the side, unconscious.

When I meet Stefano's eyes, I'm ready. But he only nods.

And I wonder, not for the first time, about his relationship with his father.

My own castigates me in irritated tones as we walk to our respective cars, but I don't give a fuck.

There's only one thing I care about right now.

And I break every single fucking speed limit in the Tri-state area getting back to her.

Caterina

There will be a reckoning for tonight.

Danny is silent in the car, but I can feel his eyes on me. Tugging my skirt down as far as it will go, I curl up on the seat, shivering. When heat blasts through despite the warm evening, I blink back tears. "Thank you."

"Sure, Cat." His voice is quiet. "You okay?"

"Fine."

My voice breaks, and I clamp down. I push down every bit of emotion riding me, shoving it into the overflowing box in my head and locking that shit down.

I just need to get home. Home, behind the walls of my apartment.

When we stop, I don't wait for Danny to open the car door. Don't wait for the Crows to check the area. Blindly, I climb out, almost stumbling in my heels. I head straight for my front door as curses echo behind me. The sound makes me flinch, and I bite down on my lip until I taste blood, undoing the locks and slipping inside.

For once, I check every single lock without being told.

Then I check it again.

And when I'm finally, finally alone, I bury my face in my hands and let it out.

Just for an hour. One single, solitary fucking hour to let my guard down before I have to build it back up again.

I don't know how long it is before the knock comes at my door.

Three hard, solid knocks. Familiar knocks.

And the relief threatens to cut me off at the knees as I scramble to my feet, my hands fighting to get the locks undone before he's pushing the door open, his hands on my face.

"I'm here," he says urgently, searching my face. "You're okay. Tell me what happened, baby."

The words spill out in shaking judders. His hands rub up and down my arms, flexing as I stumble towards the moment that Salvatore Asante thought he could put his hands on me and get away with it.

But I can't say it.

Dom studies my face. "Okay," he whispers. "It's okay, Cat. You don't have to."

Instead, he carefully wraps his arms around me, and I curl myself into him, burying my face in his neck and taking deep, heaving breaths like his scent might chase away the cold inside my chest.

When the door knocks, I can't stop the flinch. Dom looks down at me, his brows dipping before he looks to the door. "It's Dante. He won't come in unless you want him to."

"No." My throat aches. "I need to know what happened after I left. Let him in. Just... give me a minute."

When I glance in the mirror, smeared make-up greets me, and I reach for my remover. It comes off in thick, dark smudges against the cotton pads, until my reflection stares back at me, pale and wan. I progress from my make-up to my teeth, scrubbing them twice.

I still don't feel clean.

So I switch the shower on, yanking off the blazer and pulling the hem of my fitted black shirt out of my waistband, peeling it off along with my bra. But when my hand moves to the zip at the side of my skirt, I pause.

"Caterina."

I whirl, hands reaching up to cover my stomach and breasts at the low voice. "Fucking *Christ*, Dante. Breathe louder."

The tone feels normal, but his expression... I've never seen it before.

Slowly, he moves towards me. "Are you alright?"

I search his face.

"No," I say finally. "But I will be. It could have been worse."

Anger flashes across his face, darkening his eyes. "It shouldn't have happened at all."

No. it shouldn't.

I startle when Dante drops down to one knee. His hand moves to my zip. "Want this off?"

When I nod, he carefully unzips me. The skirt slips over my hips, pooling around my ankles.

Then he carefully nudges my leg open, his eyes checking my face, searching for approval before he looks down.

His eyes close, his breathing ragged. "I should have killed him."

I turn my leg. The skin is already mottled with the beginnings of what promises to be some nasty bruising, and several small but deep cuts, courtesy of his nails, leave little trails of blood smeared across my skin.

"He won't forget in a hurry," I say quietly. He'll never have the same movement in that hand again, and I'm glad for it.

Dante rests his forehead against my leg. "Shower," he says gruffly. "Take your time. Rossi is getting the first aid kit."

"It's just a few cuts. I don't need it."

It's not the physical damage I'm struggling with.

Dante gets to his feet. "I'll be outside, if you need anything."

My mouth opens as he leaves. "You can stay. In the apartment, I mean."

He looks at me over his shoulder. I don't know what he sees in my face, but his own softens. "Alright."

He's in the living room when I emerge a while later, seated across from Domenico. Their low voices pause as they both look at me. My wet hair trails down my back, and I double check the knot on my robe before I take a seat next to Dom on the couch.

"What happened?" I ask Dante. "When I... when I left."

I shouldn't be surprised. My father... he stopped protecting me a long time ago. But the hurt still creeps in when he tells me. "I see."

When he clears his throat, my eyes flash to him. "What else?"

"I... smashed his face into the table. Asante, I mean. Knocked him out."

Beside me, Dom stirs, begrudging approval in his voice. "Good."

But my lips press together. "You shouldn't have done that, Dante."

I'm already in enough shit with my father, without trying to explain why an heir would take it upon himself to defend me in any way. Dante's lips twist. "I know."

He doesn't say anything else, doesn't apologize. And maybe I don't want him to. Because at least he *did* something.

But it makes things complicated.

Resting my head back against the leather, I turn it to look at Dom. He's frowning at the floor, and I reach out to nudge him with my foot. "You're going to have more wrinkles than an elephant if you keep frowning like that, Domenico."

His lips move into an approximation of a smile, but it's forced as hell. We should talk about his trip home, but Dante's presence makes that more complicated.

Chewing on my lip, I contemplate the strangeness of having them both here, in the same space. Acting civil. "Should we... swap some memes or something?"

Dom looks at me like I've grown a third head, but Dante's eyes narrow at me. Shrugging, I reach for the remote.

"Or not. A movie it is, then."

I flick through the options, settling on a big-budget action film with lots of guns. Dom shifts, dragging a cushion down onto his lap. "Lie down."

I pull my damp hair into a braid before I settle down. Dom's fingers trace over my forehead, soft, gentle strokes, and I blink drowsily.

I doubt I'll sleep much tonight either, but maybe I can get an hour now. My eyes land on Dante's face, and just for a second, I see the envy as he watches Dom. The yearning.

When I wake up a few hours later, Dom is asleep, his hand tangled in my hair. But my feet are propped up on Dante's lap, his hand curled around my ankle. An old comedy show plays on low volume in the background but his eyes aren't on it. They're on my door. Alert. Watching.

It doesn't take much for my eyes to close again.

And this time, I don't wake up until morning.

Caterina

Today is not going to be a good day.

I can feel it in the way my head throbs as I emerge from the bedroom, Dom handing me a coffee. I glance around, but the room is otherwise empty.

"He had to go." Dom watches me from under lowered brows. "Said he'll check in later."

"There's no need. I'm fine."

Leaning against the counter, I meet his look with one of my own. My leg aches, the bruising deepening into purple, almost black splodges of damage. But I've had far worse than that. "Stop looking at me like that, Domenico. Tell me what's happening."

The feel of Asante's hands on me isn't going away anytime soon. That violation. But I don't have the headspace to waste any time on that piece of shit.

And as Dom begins to speak, that headspace gets even smaller. Until there is no space at all but for the rushing in my head.

That *motherfucker*.

"*Figlio di puttana*," I hiss. The Italian rolls off my tongue as I pace up and down. "I knew it. Evil, raping piece of *shit*."

I knew something was wrong. Knew my father was more withdrawn than usual, even after what happened this year. And it's because that asshole is whispering in his fucking ear, making me look weak at every opportunity.

And thanks to my own fucking choices, my father is starting to believe him.

"He cannot have the Crows," I snap. My throat threatens to close up at the thought. To lose my position as Corvo heir... I've spent my whole life working for that. I have sacrificed *everything* to be where I am.

Without the Crows, I don't know who I would be. But I wouldn't be me, wouldn't be Caterina Corvo. And for it to be Matteo, of all people. My stomach revolts at the sheer fucking thought of that man taking control.

None of us would be safe, could ever sleep soundly at night with him leading us. He is not stable, not *normal*.

"What the hell is my father thinking? He's a psychopath." I stare at Domenico wildly. "Look what he did to Nicoletta!"

In any other family, the punishment would have been severe. But my father not only permitted it, but *rewarded* it.

"Has he always been this way?" I ask quietly, sinking down on a chair. "My father, I mean. Am I only just seeing it?"

When Dom hesitates, I rub at my eyes. "So... that's a yes."

He settles next to me. "Maybe you're the one that's changed, Cat."

When I look at him questioningly, he leans on the table with his elbows. "You've always been so focused on the Crows. Nobody would ever question your loyalty. Your father never needed to worry about you because you never looked up, never questioned any of his decisions. You did what he needed you to do."

Hurt echoes inside my chest. "So what are you saying?"

"I am *saying*," he pokes my arm. "That the blinkers are off, Cat. You have been blind to your father's faults because he is your father, and you love him. You knew he was challenging, but you were never challenged *by* him because he never needed to. But now... now you're seeing more clearly. Hell, we're graduating this year. You were always going to find your feet, and now that you have, I don't think you like what you see. And he can sense that."

Sitting next to him, I think over his words. And they make sense.

I *have* changed.

"You're right," I say finally, my voice hoarse.

And maybe... maybe that means that I'm not the best person to lead the Crows.

When I voice the thoughts to Dom, though, he stiffens. "That's what you took from that conversation? Fucking hell, Cat. You think any of us here would follow anyone else? *Matteo*?"

He spits out my cousin's name like poison. My phone vibrates on the counter, and when I pick it up, my lips press together. "Well, maybe I can have a little chat with him today."

Because my father is summoning me home.

Despite Dom's furious protestations, he gets smaller behind me in the rearview mirror as I leave him behind.

The breath leaves me in a sigh of relief as I pull through the campus gates, the sleek red Corvette idling in a gentle purr beneath my hands before I hit the gas.

The Corvo estate is more than an hour away, and the minutes tick away too quickly. It's with regret that I pull up to our ornate but secure outer gates. They open silently, the security staff recognising my car, and I wind through the grounds.

I always loved this place. Loved the lush, green outdoors, acres and acres of space to lose myself in with childhood games. Loved the little stream that winds its way through, where Aldo taught me to catch trout with sharpened sticks, the rocks sharp beneath my feet as I waited patiently for hours to get the right moment to strike.

But as the house comes into view, the majestic colonial design similar to that of the Cosa Nostra meeting place but with impossibly more ornate decoration, the nostalgia fades away. My last memories from this place... no. I will not think about those today.

There's no trace of discomfort in my posture, nothing for anyone to remark on as I emerge, tossing my keys to the valet and walking in as though every part of me isn't on alert.

No, I walk in exactly as I am. The Corvo heir, coming home.

I'm met with familiar faces. My father likes routine, doesn't trust easily. Many of the staff here are people I've known my entire life. They keep their heads down as they pass, some offering a nod and a murmured welcome before they continue in their tasks.

The atmosphere here has changed. The staff scurry, rather than walk. As if they're keeping their heads down.

"Miss Caterina." Turning, I offer the short, portly man a smile. Our butler has worked here for longer than I've been alive. He was, by all accounts, devoted to my mother before she died. A dedicated man, but not an overly friendly one. His bow is deep. "Welcome back. Your father is waiting in the study."

"Thank you, Fernandez. I'll take some coffee, please."

Truthfully, I'd prefer alcohol, but it's barely lunchtime. Fernandez disappears as I stroll through the house. It's quiet. I'm used to seeing men in and out, some gathering in the many rooms we have here. But today, the house is silent.

The deep, walnut-colored door is closed when I reach it. Knocking, I'm met with silence.

No. not silence. Someone shifts inside, the light creak of my father's battered leather chair sounding as he leans back. I can see it in my mind, such a familiar sight I could probably sketch it from memory, even though my drawing skills are lackluster, at best.

I wait. Still and silent. And I wait.

So, this is how it's going to be.

My father has always played these games. Enjoyed keeping people waiting, their nerves building as they wonder why. He taught me the trick years ago.

He's never used it on me before.

Finally, his voice filters through. "Enter."

I wait a few seconds rather than immediately opening the door. When I push it open, Joseph Corvo is exactly where I knew he would be. He doesn't look up, his pen scratching at a piece of the paperwork scattered across his oak desk.

When the door knocks, I stride over and pull it open without waiting for approval, taking the tray from a visibly surprised Fernandez and carrying it over to a side table. "Coffee, father?"

The chair creaks again. I can feel him watching me, but I keep my back turned, pouring out the freshly-brewed coffee and adding a splash of milk. Turning, I place a cup down on his desk before taking a seat in the dark green leather Chesterfield opposite. The wide bay window behind him offers a beautiful view of the gardens whilst shadowing his face, making it difficult to make out the nuances of his expression.

Undoubtedly intentional.

He glances at the cup. "I prefer to take it with sugar."

"Stop. It's bad for your heart." Sipping at the drink, I wait.

Finally, he snorts out a laugh, picking up the cup. "I must be getting old, to allow my daughter to dictate my coffee order."

"Only because you know I'm right."

The cup clatters as he puts it down. "I wish to discuss last night."

And just like that, the father disappears. Replaced with the don. The fondness wipes from his face as he waits for my response.

"By all means. What part in particular would you like to discuss?"

He clasps his fists together. "Let us start with your behavior. It was out of line."

My back draws up, my spine a straight line. "Unusual, perhaps. But out of line, I would disagree with. Strongly."

He slaps his hand against the table. "You stabbed our biggest ally in the hand. To say nothing of your rudeness in interrupting the meeting for the Fusco boy."

Carefully, so carefully, I choose my words. "An alliance in our world is not permission for poor behavior. I reacted accordingly. Asante needed a reminder that an alliance does not equate to weakness. If I had not responded to his actions, he would have seen it as exactly that."

I watch my father consider the words. There is no mention of anything so emotional as feelings. No mention of the violation I felt as his hand slid up my skin with every intention of touching my most intimate parts.

In this room, there is only space for politics. Feelings do not matter.

"It made us look disjointed," he counters. "Something we cannot afford. The Cosa Nostra is fractured enough. Our enemies are no longer only on the outside."

"It showed that we will take action against any threat. No matter where it originates," I counter, my voice firm. "We do not bend to the whims of others. My priority is the Corvo name, and I will not allow us to show weakness. To *anyone*. Ally or not."

My voice remains even, my face showing none of the turbulence flipping my stomach inside out.

"His hand will never be the same again." My father reaches for his coffee, sipping. "He was not happy."

"Neither was I," I respond quietly. "And yet you make no mention of that."

I cannot stop it, the brief admonishment. A verbal acknowledgement that I see his response, and I find it lacking.

He sighs. "Caterina. We have had many discussions over the years. You are the first female heir. That comes with a set of challenges I have never had to face. You have assured me at every turn that this would never be a problem. And yet, here we are."

The heat suffuses my cheeks. "It is not a *problem*," I force out. "I responded to a threat. If Asante had attacked you physically, you would have responded in a similar vein. And presuming Asante takes my warning for the truth it is, it will never be a problem again."

"And what about the next man?" he asks directly. "It will be a problem then, no?"

Realization hits.

There is nothing I can say to him. He will twist my words, throw them back at me, use last night to make me look like a hysterical fucking *female*.

"You are not looking for answers," I say quietly. "Nothing I can say will make a difference here. You're searching for an excuse. Why?"

I see the admission on his face, even as he tries to twist it back on me. "I am simply trying to establish how you plan to proceed, Caterina. This may be the first time, but I doubt it will be the last. Will you stab every man in the hand?"

"Not every man is a would-be rapist," I say coldly. "Although we do seem to have an additional stock of them at the moment. How *is* Matteo?"

"We are not talking about Matteo. We are talking about you."

"How long do you intend to punish me?"

My abrupt switch sees him flounder, his eyes flickering. "I don't understand."

Leaning forward, I look into his eyes. "You taught me these games, Joseph. Let us not waste either of our time on them. You are punishing me for what happened. What's done is done. That part of my life is *over*. It has no bearing on last night."

He only looks at me. "I'm not punishing you."

The laugh is a sharp one, disbelieving. "Tell me. Am I still the Corvo heir?"

Silence. An enduring, deep emptiness that sends an icy blade into my stomach.

Finally, he speaks. "I am not punishing you, Caterina. That you believe I am tells me that despite all of your training, all of the effort I have invested in you, you are still not ready. You ask if you are still the Corvo heir? Yes. For now. But I will not allow weakness into our ranks. And that is all I am seeing. Distraction after distraction, all of it taking away from what we need to be focusing on. Growth. Strength. This is what is important. Not these damn petty squabbles."

The lecturing tone of his words grates on me. Gritting my teeth, I force my head to nod slowly. "I quite agree. As I said, what's done is done. Last night was unfortunate."

"Not just because of Asante. Our traditions are important. You spoke out of turn."

I settle back in my chair, confident in my response. "Because there was no need to torture an already broken man. A waste of everyone's time and energy. Where is the strength in that? Let the Fusco boy pick up the slack. It may distract him from... other thoughts."

My father acknowledges the truth in my words with a wave of his hand. "Perhaps. And yet *il bacio della morte* sits upon your head, and I see you taking no action to address it. How many attempts have you seen?"

"Only three. None of them successful."

"That is beyond the point," he snaps. "Three *now*. It's been a bare handful of days. In the weeks, months, *years* to come, they will only grow. Fusco is playing the long game with nothing to lose, or so he thinks. He knows that eventually you will get tired.

"The attempts will wear you down. You will either be forced into hiding, or you will be dead. And you wonder why I have reservations about your future? Why I may need to make other arrangements?"

My fist clenches on the arm of the chair. "As you said, it has only been days. Do not scoff at the small amount of time that has passed and in the same breath slate me for not stopping it. *Il bacio della morte* is not so easy to remove. It has never *been* removed once given. Persuading Giovanni will take time. And in the meantime, I will not allow them to wear me down. And I will certainly not make it easy for them."

"You will use the other sister."

His words sink like a stone in the space between us.

Rosa Fusco. Her face appears in my mind, grieving and angry and *young*. So fucking young, but no longer as innocent as her sister was.

The rejection rises on my tongue, and my father points at me. "No fucking arguments, Caterina. You will use the Fusco sister to move things along. If you want to consider it a test, then it's a fucking test. Matteo did what needed to be done to break the father."

He drops his hand. "You will do what is needed to break the son."

Because it would break Gio, if he lost another sister. He's barely holding himself together as it is, jagged, angry pieces of grief. If he lost Rosa too—

The Fusco line would be finished. Ripe for the vultures to come along and pick at the leftovers.

"Do this, and your place as heir is secure." My father stands and opens the door for me to leave. "Fail, and I *will* consider an alternative, daughter."

I stand, sweeping past him. I don't respond.

"I will visit you soon," he says behind me. "I find myself curious to see how the campus has changed since I was last there."

Not a goodbye, as the door closes behind me.

A threat.

Caterina

Swearing, I dig my palms into my eyes. All I can see is numbers across the back of my eyelids. Accounts. So many fucking accounts.

But none of them are the *right* accounts.

The Corvos specialize in financial crime. We can get rid of any dirty money, turn it into neatly stacked piles of clean, cold cash. We can also create money where it's needed. With that comes a specific set of subskills. Namely, *hacking*.

Stretching, I give myself a break from the screens in front of me and pour another coffee, ignoring the jitters in my chest telling me I've had far too much damn caffeine for the day. I've been holed up in my office at the Corvo building since I returned from my meeting with my father. Searching for a way to escape the ultimatum held over my head.

The order to use a young girl to break the Fusco family in brutal, horrific finality.

In our world, money is everything. Power. Prestige. A statement.

Without it, you have nothing. No voice. Certainly no way of paying your dues.

If I can just find my way into the Fusco accounts, I can manipulate them. Move them. Empty them, if I have to.

It all depends on how willing Giovanni is to negotiate, once his money is in my hands.

But the Fuscos aren't stupid. None of the families of the Cosa Nostra are. Everyone has their accounts locked up, layer upon layer of the best security the money and influence of the American mafia can buy. Watertight, for all but the most experienced specialists. An important protective measure when your competitors are the best there fucking is.

My hacking skills are decent. More than decent, really. But the more I try to work my way around the edges, to softly peel back layer after layer after damned layer, the more frustrated I get. You can't do this kind of work without patience. And today, I'm all fucking out of it.

The tentative knock on the door only annoys me more. I ducked out of training, opting to skip my schedule for the day in favor of locking myself in here and trying to fix what feels like a fucking unfixable issue. And I gave Tony strict instructions not to let any fucker through.

"What?" I snap, pulling open the door. And then I pause.

Stefano Asante fills the doorway. He's so damn tall that his head nearly brushes against the doorframe as he blocks out the light. Dressed in a smart black sweater and dark jeans, he keeps his hands in his pockets as he flicks his eyes towards me and then away. "If this isn't a good time, I can leave."

Silently, I stand back, and he ducks into the room. He doesn't speak as he looks around, taking in the empty desk, the screens. I settle back into my chair and reach out to power them off. "Why are you here?"

He's never been here. In fact, I don't think I've ever seen him outside of the common areas or our combined sessions as heirs. The Asantes tend to keep to themselves, their section of campus over on the other side.

They don't court trouble, almost as silent as their leader. On campus, at least.

Stefano turns back to look at me. His deep brown eyes are so dark, they bleed into the pupils. "I came to see if you were alright."

His words, the deep, bass tones of his voice, make my skin tighten. Low, almost gentle.

Like I'm a *victim*. My hackles almost fly up.

"Fine," I say coldly. "I'd ask how Salvatore is, but I honestly couldn't give a fuck."

Unless he was on the verge of a painful death. Then I'd probably celebrate. Unfortunately, he's unlikely to die from the wound I gave him.

For a moment, Stefano's mouth tilts up in amusement. But it soon disappears.

"You need to be careful," he says quietly. "He will not forget this, Caterina."

My eyes narrow. "And yet you're here, warning me about your own father."

He glances towards the window. "We do not choose our family. And nobody would choose to be his enemy if they knew what he was capable of."

It's a little dramatic, to be honest. "We're the mafia, Stefano. I'd say we're all capable of being the big bad wolf."

He frowns. "He is much more than that. I came to warn you. It's up to you what you do with it. And... I wanted to apologize. It shouldn't have happened."

"Well, it did." I gesture towards the door. "I appreciate the apology, Stefano. Truly. But if your father wants to come for me again, I'll have my knives ready. He doesn't scare me."

Salvatore can join the fucking queue. It seems to be growing by the day.

I call Tony in when Stefano leaves as silently as he arrived, still a little bemused by the encounter. "Did I or did I not say I wasn't to be disturbed?"

Tony shifts. "Apologies, Cat. When it's an heir, it's hard to say no. Easy to cause offense and all that. He left his weapons with us."

Huh. My eyebrows rise at the information. "So when Giovanni Fusco comes to call, you'll just wave him through? Good to know."

Tony looks up quickly. "That's different. The Asantes are allies."

Sighing, I nearly wave him out, but an idea strikes. "Do we have any particularly talented hackers in the current intake? The newest arrivals, I mean."

He frowns. "I think we might. Vincent would be best to ask."

It makes sense, given that he has the overall responsibility for them. "Find out. Tell him to send any possibilities to me."

"Will do." He stays where he is, and I glance back up. "You can leave now."

A fruitless afternoon passes as I continue working, but I'm no closer to finding an entry point when I finally pack up. Night is starting to settle in as I leave, heading towards the dining hall. I'm lost in my own thoughts, still mentally working through patterns, possible options.

The hit is sudden. Something rough wraps around my neck, violently tugging, yanking me off my feet and dragging me backwards as I choke, taken off guard by the pain. Thuds and grunts echo around me as I try desperately to shove my fingers between the rope and my skin.

Strangulation is not a death I would choose. If I can't get a hold before they hit my carotid or my jugular, I'm dead.

It feels like I struggle for hours, and dark begins to creep in at the edges of my vision.

I'm losing. Unconsciousness beckons, a heavy, full sensation that weakens my limbs as my arm starts to drop.

An angry shout, and my body folds like a marionette, collapsing into the ground. The darkness recedes as I gasp, limbs shaking violently as I suck in breath.

"Cat – Cat!"

Tony is white as he shakes my shoulders. I think he's on his knees, can see the last of the fight behind him, figures darting in and out of the trees. "Jesus – help!"

I shake my head, trying to clear the buzzing as more voices join, more faces stare down at me. "Did you get them?"

They stare, and I try to say it again. "Did you get them?"

The words don't sound right. Garbled and strange, like each word is too long to fit inside my mouth. But Tony understands. "We got them. Two dead. One down."

Three.

That's not very fucking fair.

I hold up five fingers. "Give... me—,"

"Clear the space!" Tony bellows. "Get Domenico. Nobody in or out."

His fingers gently probe at the broken skin at my neck, and he hisses between his teeth. "This looks really bad. You need a hospital."

My head shakes. "F-four."

Four minutes. Four minutes of focusing on forcing the air in and out, of adjusting to the pain in my neck. The numbness in my limbs recedes, replaced by a burning sensation.

"Your eyes, Cat," Tony whispers shakily. "They – the blood vessels—,"

I nod to show my understanding. His face becomes a little clearer.

I feel... broken. Like maybe I do need a hospital.

But there's something else I have to do first.

My four minutes vanish too soon. "Help... me up."

There's barely any volume to my rasping voice. Tony goes to lift me, but someone else gets there first.

"I've got you," Dom murmurs. He slides his hands under me, and I'm not sure if the shaking is from me or from him. "Steady."

As he gently lifts me, holding me up, I regret trying to move. I fold in half, retching, as Dom gathers my hair. Liquid spatters across the hard, packed ground courtesy of my caffeine diet. Biting back a whimper at the pain in my throat, I straighten. Tony looks away from me, as if embarrassed.

And now I'm *really* fucking angry.

"Where?" I ask – whisper – and Tony nods behind me. With Dom's help, I take a few shaky steps, testing my balance. I'm going to need it.

When the pins and needle recede, I tap on his arm. "Ok."

He releases me without question, and I slowly walk over to where the Fusco solider kneels on the ground. The barrel of a gun presses against the side of his head, and he spits at the ground when he sees me. The noose he used to drag me across the floor is in front of him. "Fucking devil bitch. Why won't you just die?"

I feel like I might topple over, so I stay where I am. "Sorry to disappoint."

The bodies of the two men who attacked mine lie next to him, and his eyes keep landing on them, bouncing away. "Go on, then."

He expects me to kill him.

I hold out my hand, and someone presses a gun into it. Curling my finger around the trigger, I gesture. "Put the rope around your neck."

He hesitates, then. Panicked eyes darting around, as if the knowledge is sinking in. "I—,"

When I nod, Dom steps out from beside me. He picks up the rope, turning it over in his hands. There's violence in his face as he pushes it over the male's head, pulling the noose tight until he wheezes for breath. Tighter.

"Enough."

Dom loosens it immediately, and the man gasps. His eyes are bright, wet, when he looks up at me. "*Please—*,"

"Again."

He howls this time, the noise abruptly cutting off as Dom yanks it even harder. His eyes bulge, veins purpling, blood vessels bursting in the whites of his eyes.

Just like he did to me.

"Stop."

Dom hands me the end of the rope, and I tug it, drawing his attention. Spit has collected in the corner of his mouth. "Up."

There's barely any strength in my hold, but I don't need it. The rope hangs loose as he shuffles ahead, my gun providing all the incentive he needs as we march slowly towards the dining hall.

Dom stays close to me, his hand at my elbow. "You gonna make it?"

My nod is grim.

It feels like an eternity until we reach the doors. The Crows open them, silent as he drags himself through them. A little faster now. As though redemption lies ahead.

Perhaps he's remembering the men I sent back. Tied, embarrassed, but alive.

It takes a few moments for people to notice. To see the rope. The gun in my hands.

The state of my fucking face.

And then there are whispers, people standing up to see. The hall is full, and as we pass the Fusco table, someone shouts in recognition.

I ignore them, trusting in Dom and the Crows to watch my back.

I'm not in the position to fight a battle on two fronts right now. I can barely keep myself upright, but I force my back to straighten, to put one foot in front of the other.

Everyone stands as I reach the dais. Dante grips the table, his knuckles whitening. Luciano stares at my face. Even Stefano gets to his feet, his eyes moving over us coolly.

Giovanni crosses his arms, but I can see something in his expression as we reach the bottom of the steps. Surprise, maybe.

Like he didn't expect me to survive.

The man crashes down to his knees. I can see him shaking, see his shoulders curve inwards. I walk up behind him, press my gun to the back of his neck, and I look Giovanni Fusco in the eyes.

"Remember who lit the match," I rasp. His face tightens.

And then I pull the trigger.

Blood sprays across the steps, blood and matter, and the body slumps forward. A scream rings out from the Fusco table, and I spare a thought for those who will be grieving tonight. In the days that follow. One, single, brief thought.

It's all the empathy I have to spare right now.

It takes me longer than I'd like to walk around him. For my shoes to coat themselves in his blood as I slowly, so fucking slowly, climb the steps.

Luciano silently pulls out the empty middle seat, and I slide into it, my neck aching. I place my gun in front of me.

My eyes scan the silent hall.

Nobody meets my stare.

Not even the Fuscos.

Not as I slowly work my way through the meal Dom brings me, his face hard. He knows better than to bring me something soft, even as my stomach tightens in dread at the sight of it. Every bite is accompanied by burning, savage pain as I try to eat.

But I clear my whole fucking plate.

And when I walk out again, every single Crow standing and following in my wake, all I leave behind me is silence and death.

CATERINA

"Tell Gio I want a meeting."

My throat still burns, and I'm not sure if Dom hears me. He continues packing away the medical kit, tossing the used alcohol pads into the trash. I stare at the plain white ceiling from my position on the couch, my fingers prodding at the ligature burns on my neck.

"Stop that," he says gruffly. Capturing my hand with his, he keeps hold of it as he settles down on the floor beside me, his head leaning against my stomach.

Slowly, my other hand reaches down, brushing across his soft, inky hair. His sigh is closer to a shudder.

"I thought I'd lost you today," he murmurs. "When they called me, I heard the shouting in the background... I thought you were dead, Cat."

I let my fingers delve into the softness of his cropped hair, trace the shaved edges. "Still here. I'm not quite that easy to kill, you know."

His hand tightens around mine. "I can't lose you. It was too close."

Something dangerously close to vulnerability fills his voice.

The door knocks, and he closes his eyes with a groan. "Fucking V'Arezzo."

He gets up with a grumble. But it's not Dante at the door.

My eyes widen when Luc strides in, his hazel eyes landing on mine. He scans my face, my neck, and his face tightens. "Little crow."

I try to lift myself up, but his hand lands on my shoulder, gently stopping it. "Don't get up. You look halfway to dead, in case you hadn't realized."

"Oh, I realized."

Dom catches my eye, tilting his head towards the door in a silent question, and I shake my head. He lifts his eyes up, as if he's asking the heavens for patience, before he disappears into the kitchen.

Luc raises his eyebrows as an irritated bang sounds. "Domenico Rossi is very protective of you, you know."

"That goes both ways. Why are you here, Luc?"

He twists one way, then the other. Then he shrugs. As if he's not quite sure himself. "You've had a fucking shit few days. I just wanted to check in. Make sure you're still the savage little crow I enjoy verbally and physically sparring with."

My snort of amusement fucking hurts. "No changes here, you'll be glad to know."

"Good."

I blink as he drops an envelope on my stomach. "Another gift?"

"Not quite," he says softly. "There is something to be said about privacy in our line of work, Caterina. Complete, utter privacy. There is one, single place on campus that nobody else knows about. Aside from me, that is. There is a key and directions in the envelope. I thought you might appreciate the notion of somewhere you can't be disturbed because technically, it does not *exist*."

His words wash through me. "Why would you share this with me?"

Because this is a gift.

Everywhere we go, we are watched. People always want something from the heirs. A moment of our time, a question, a complaint, a proposal. To have somewhere nobody knows about, to know that the door isn't being watched, that nobody is waiting outside to hurt me—

Yes, that is a gift.

His face turns serious. "Because I know you will not betray it. And I find that I wouldn't mind sharing this space with you, little crow. Just lock the door behind you, and I'll know that it's occupied. The same applies."

Nodding, I pick up the envelope, studying my name, written in a flawless script on the front. Steel myself to ask a question, one of many on the tip of my tongue. It takes me longer than I thought it would. "Luc... about the daggers."

But when I look up, he's already gone.

Luciano

I nearly kick Dante V'Arezzo in the ribs as I leave. He looks just as startled as I am, sitting on his ass outside my little crow's front door. "What the hell are you doing here, Morelli?"

Surveying him, I tilt my head. "I could ask you the same question."

He huffs, but he doesn't respond. Choosing to keep my own counsel, I glance around. The copse of trees outside Caterina's apartment sway in the breeze, leaves gently rustling. "Looks like it's going to rain."

He stays silent, and I blink, assessing him with new eyes. Taking in the gun balanced across his legs. "You're staying out here. All night?"

That doesn't sound like the Dante V'Arezzo I know.

The glare is glacial. "In case you hadn't noticed, there's a fucking death sentence over her head."

Oh, I noticed. Haven't thought about much else the last few days.

Caterina Corvo is taking up far too much space inside my head.

But then, that's nothing new.

My fingers curl into a fist, the image of her battered, rope-burned neck permanently etched into my memories. And probably my nightmares, too. "If there's a rota, you can put my name down."

I don't know who's more surprised at the words. Dante opens his mouth, then closes it again. "Speak to Rossi. He's co-ordinating."

Domenico Rossi. The protector. Of course he is.

My laugh is soft, and Dante glances up at me in silent question. "Who'd have thought it? Our first female heir, and here we all are, panting after her."

It's as close to a confession as I'm willing to give, especially to him.

He leans his head back against the railing. "It's not because she's the first."

No, it's not. There is something about Caterina Corvo, something magnetic. As if she's the fucking sun, and we're all just circling her orbit.

Helpless to resist.

It's not a feeling I'm used to. I like control, obsess over having it in every aspect of my life. But with her... I have none. No control at all.

"Well, then," I say softly, stepping over him. "May the best man win, V'Arezzo."

Fighting words, but as I stroll away, I know the truth. It sticks to me like ashes, follows me everywhere.

There's not a chance in hell that Caterina Corvo will ever choose me.

It already happened once.

And I fucking blew it.

CATERINA

I stare down at the dead crow at my feet, crumpled and broken.

And then at the next one.

A trail of them, in fact, leading all the way down the path I take every morning towards the dining hall. "How imaginative."

Dom grunts, reaching out to poke one with his foot. "We need to switch up your routine. I'll get these cleaned up."

He pulls out his phone, but my hand lands on his arm. "No."

My lip curls, but my voice is little more than a croak. "I have another idea."

The dining hall is quiet this morning, just a handful of people dotted around. My eyes land on the Crow table. Amie glances up and pauses. Her eyes slide down, to the vicious-looking marks around my neck.

"I've been trying to get hold of you for days." Sliding into the seat opposite, I wait for Dom to bring breakfast over. When he slides the bowl in front of me, I glare down at the plain yogurt and drizzle of honey like it's a personal insult.

Of all the things he could have picked.

Amie glances at me and then away. "Sorry. I've been... it's been busy."

Her voice is cool, and I frown. "Are you okay?"

She shakes her head, and an awkward look makes its way onto her face. "I should be asking you that. Your neck... it looks painful."

"It is," I admit. More than I'm letting on. I've dosed myself up with maximum painkillers, but it's not enough to do more than slightly dampen the burning.

She doesn't respond, and I stare down into my bowl. This... this feels awkward. Uncomfortable. And I have absolutely no idea why that would be the case.

"Was everything okay the other night?" I ask abruptly, and she looks confused. "When the guys took you home?"

"Oh – yeah. They were fine." She laughs. "Man, I was tanked."

I blink as she stands up from the table. "You haven't finished your food."

She shrugs. "Yeah. I have a full day. See you."

I turn to watch as she walks off, my fingers tapping on the table until someone slides into her vacated seat. Alessandro's eyes widen as he gets a good look at my neck. "Oh, shit. I mean – uh—,"

"Spit it out," I mutter, and he reddens. "Sorry. I, um. I'm *in*."

My eyes fly back up to his grinning face.

Finally, some *good* news. It's about fucking time I caught a break. My eyes almost close in relief, and I can't help but grin back at him, even if it makes my neck ache more. It probably looks grotesque, thanks to the popped blood vessels in my eyes. To his credit, he only cringes a little.

"I'm impressed. Thanks, Sandro. Meet me at my office in... three hours? That work for you?"

I abandon my shitty horrible yogurt. Life is too short to eat food that looks and tastes like it belongs in a fucking prison. Vincent and Tony are following me around today, another two younger Crows with them, and they walk me over to the building where we have our law lectures. Or, as Lorena likes to call them, our *goddamn fucking common sense* lectures.

Every session, I like her a little more. It's just me and Stefano today. Dom is off picking up some of the work he's been forced to put aside in his role as chief babysitter, and I have no idea where the others are. I'm just glad to be spared the hell of hours in a room with Gio Fusco.

Lorena stomps in a good fifteen minutes later, coffee in hand. She pauses to take in my face, a low whistle escaping her painted lips. "They still alive?"

I hold her gaze. "No."

She clicks her tongue. "Didn't think they would be."

Her voice almost sounds like approval, and my chin lifts as she launches into a story about the art world that I find myself engrossed in. With their focus on money laundering and fraud through art and high-class forgeries, Luc would *definitely* find it useful.

I add a few more notes to the page. Not that I plan on sharing them with him.

Probably not.

Dom is leaning against the wall, his eyes scanning our surroundings as I exit. Stefano ducks around us without speaking, and I watch as his back disappears down the hall. "You ready?"

"My office next. I need to meet with Sandro."

"He found a way in?" When I nod, Dom lets out a breath. "Shit, Cat. This whole fucking shitshow could be done by dinner."

It's a nice thought, but I wonder if it could possibly be that easy.

I just hope it is.

For his sake.
And for mine.

Caterina

The Courtyard is neutral ground. Our *only* neutral ground, agreed and shaken on by each of the five dons. We are not permitted to harm another person within its boundary. If it wouldn't be seen as weak, I could spend all day, every day, here, dump myself here with a fucking tent and a blow-up mattress and nobody would be able to challenge it, *il bacio della morte* be damned.

Dom even suggested it, despite knowing as well as I do that I would lose every bit of respect I've earned over the years for such a cowardly move.

The space immediately around it, though, that's fair game.

The attempt is sloppy as hell. I hear him coming from at least ten paces, his breathing uneven, feet crunching through leaves. Dom tenses, but I step away from him and draw my dagger from my sleeve, keeping it in front of me.

He throws himself out from behind a fucking bush. The yell catches in his throat as I spin, and his throat lands directly on my pointed blade, sliding into it as easily as a well-cooked steak. His face contorts into a grotesque gurgle, as though he can't quite understand what's happening. A line of blood makes its way out of the corner of his lips, still dripping as I yank the dagger back with vague disgust.

"That was fucking terrible," I croak as he collapses. "Does nobody have any fucking style?"

A slow clapping makes me turn. Giovanni Fusco stands in the center of the Courtyard, alone. He lowers his hands, and there's not a shred of care in him for his man, lying dead at my feet. "Gio. I'm beginning to get a little concerned about the quality of your current intake."

"Glory hunters," he says, spreading his hands. "But they serve their purpose."

Ah, yes. Of course.

Wearing me down. Physically. Mentally.

And then, when I start to stumble, to tire of the constant watching, the real attempts will begin. And the hunt starts in earnest.

Wonderful.

Matching his movement, I spread my own arms in invitation. "I'm right here. Care to try your hand?"

Dom almost vibrates with tension when I tilt my head, silently telling him to get back.

This is between me and the man who strolls across the Courtyard towards me.

"Not quite yet," he murmurs, his eyes moving to my neck. "But soon. I'll have my pound of flesh from you, Caterina. And we have plenty of time."

"Fine." Dropping my arms, I take a step over the invisible line until I'm standing on the cobbled stone. "I have a proposition for you."

"I have no interest in negotiation," he says, his tone bored. "Is that all?"

Standing my ground, I lift my chin up. "You'll have an interest in this one. I was sorry to hear of your financial difficulties."

For the first time, I see a crack. "What difficulties."

His voice is flat, but there's something there. I choose my words carefully.

If I'm not careful, I have a feeling I won't leave here without a bullet in my skull and fuck neutral ground. A feeling that Giovanni Fusco would rather go down in a hail of bullets than concede a single damn thing to my family.

So for once, I do the opposite of what I've always been taught.

Never show weakness.

"I don't want this, Gio," I whisper. His eyes sharpen. "I'm tired of watching people die. And I know you don't want to hear it, but I'm sorry. So fucking sorry about Nicoletta."

The pain crosses his face. "Shut up."

"I'm not afraid to die," I force out through my aching throat. "None of us expect to live long lives. But killing me will not bring *her* back. It will only start another circle of war, Gio, and you will lose *everything*. If you would just recon—"

"*I have already lost everything!*"

His roar makes me step back; the bellow so full of agony that I wonder how the fuck he's still walking around. "You have no fucking idea what you've done. You and your poisonous fucking family have ripped mine apart, and I will not stop until you are all dead, Caterina. You and that *cunt* of a cousin that dares to call himself a man."

His chest heaves, up and down, and a flicker of fear appears in my stomach. The rules don't matter, right now. There are no rules.

He will kill me, and I'm not sure I'll be able to stop him. Not sure even Domenico would be able to stop him.

But I have to try, as I hold my hand up.

"You still have a sister," I breathe.

And he goes still. His entire body locks up, so tight that I don't think he's even breathing.

"What. Did. You. Say."

"I have orders," I say quietly, meeting his searing gaze. "To use Rosa and make you submit, Gio."

I can see his hands shaking. "You're not touching my fucking sister, you bitch."

He's not listening. The man I knew would have read between the lines, understood the subtext. But I don't know *this* version of Giovanni Fusco.

Or maybe I never knew him at all.

"Listen to me, damn you!" My voice rises. "As of an hour ago, I have access to all the Fusco bank accounts, Gio. Every single one. All of the money – every fucking penny of it."

My words make him pause. "You just won't fucking stop, will you?"

And he sounds so damn tired that the pity threatens to shred my chest. But I hold firm.

"Call off the *il bacio della morte*. In return, I swear that I will not touch a hair on your sister's head, nor will I touch your accounts. If you call it off, and lay low for a while – that includes not pissing off my father. Don't force my fucking hand on this, Giovanni."

I take a breath. "I don't want to be here," I say finally. "Any more than you do."

His hands open and close in jerky motions. "You will not harm my sister."

"You have my word," I whisper. "I swear it, Gio. But you need to back down, and you need to do it *now*. Because I am running out of time to fix this."

His laugh is the saddest thing I've ever heard. "There is no *fixing* this."

I close my eyes briefly. "No. That was... it was a stupid choice of words. But tell me you agree, Gio."

Stiff, angry, his nod is a movement of his head, but he *nods*. "Fine. I'm not there this evening, I'll let my men know and announce it formally at breakfast tomorrow. But if you *ever* rescind your word, if my sister is harmed in any way, I'll kill you myself."

I nearly sway in relief. "Agreed."

As he turns and walks away, it feels like the world is holding its breath. I wait for the punchline.

But as Giovanni disappears from view, nothing happens.

Footsteps sound behind me, and I spin. Domenico moves slowly, but he's grinning.

"Cat," he says, almost disbelievingly. "It's done. You did it."

I clear my throat. "I guess so."

It doesn't feel like an achievement at all. There's a bad taste in my mouth, the aftermath of holding Rosa Fusco's safety over Giovanni's head.

I would never have hurt her.

But at least now, I don't have to make that decision. I don't have to *choose*.

The breath that expands my lungs feels like the first true one I've taken in days. Warm hands cup my face, fingers stroking my skin, and I zero in on Dom, on the relief shining in his eyes, lighter than I've ever seen them. He's so close that I can see the faintest specks of silver and blue in his gaze.

The gaze that dips to my lips. "Caterina."

"Domenico," I breathe. The air catches in my lungs, waiting.

All of me, waiting. Like I've been waiting forever,

But the smile on his face slips, his hands sliding away from my face. He takes a step back.

"We should go. It's time for dinner."

And I'm left to stare as he walks away from me.

He doesn't look back.

Caterina

Everyone is quiet at dinner.

So quiet, that when my stomach growls audibly, Luc turns his head to look at me incredulously. "What? I haven't eaten much today."

In fact, all I've had was that shitty yogurt. I'm starving.

Seated in what seems to be becoming my usual spot between Dante and Luciano, I glance over at the Fusco table. I'm met with angry stares, but there don't seem to be any terribly planned knife attacks heading my way.

It seems that Gio spread the word after all.

Dom turns away from speaking with Tony and climbs the stairs, placing my plate down in front of me. I pull it towards me eagerly – and then pause, staring in horror at the brown gloop awaiting me. "What... what the fuck is this?"

Dom is still chewing a mouthful of food, looking vaguely sick. "I forgot about the plan."

"What pl– *oh*."

This morning seems a lifetime away now.

"I have regrets," I whisper sadly. "So many regrets."

Dom swallows the lump of meat in his mouth. "I wouldn't risk it."

I look up at him mournfully. "They're all going to try and kill me now."

He frowns at me. "That's not even funny."

"It was a little funny," I mutter. He heads back down towards the Crows, and I pick up my fork with a sigh. "Here goes nothing."

"What did you do to the food?" Luc demands, and Dante turns to me. Stefano leans forward to look as I purse my lips.

"I thought it would be ironic," I say weakly. "To make everyone eat crow. Literally."

Specifically, the Asantes, but since we all eat the same unless we have a specific need, most of the room is now tucking into a pie made from the birds left on my doorstep.

Maybe it wasn't the best idea I've ever had.

"That's the worst fucking idea I've ever heard," Dante snaps, but Luc turns his head away, staring down the hall.

And my head snaps back as he shoves my plate, so hard that it slides over the edge and smashes against the stone floor. "Fucking hell, Morelli. It's just a *pie*."

I lean over the table to get a closer look, and my eyes catch on something up ahead. As someone shouts for help.

Dante and Luc are both out of their seats, but I shove past them.

Running.

I thought I knew fear. Knew the taste of it in my mouth, felt the chill of it in my bones.

But I was wrong.

Because I have never known fear like this.

As I land on my knees next to him, shoving Vincent out of the way, my hands tremble as I press two fingers against his pulse. Praying.

"Domenico—,"

His name pounds inside my chest, etched on every beat of my heart as he sucks in oxygen in choking, mottled breaths. His pupils are dilated, shrinking to pinpricks of black as he gasps for air. His hand claws at his neck, and the sob breaks out of me as his breathing speeds up. My hands touch his face, his chest, the panic overwhelming and violent.

Because he's dying. Domenico is dying, in front of me.

I don't know what to do. How to fix this.

"Caterina." Dante snaps my name as he kneels next to me. "We need to stabilize him. Focus."

Yes—

Dante is barking instructions, and someone passes him water and a napkin. I watch as he pours it out, soaking the cloth and wiping it over Dom's mouth.

To try and remove the poison.

"I'll do it," I force out, and he doesn't even pause. "Like fuck you will. Do the compressions."

My mind settles into cold clarity as I lock my hands together over Dom's chest. It's stopped rising now, stopped *moving*, and the panic threatens to shove back in. Because if Dom is gone—

No.

No.

"You're not dying on me, Domenico Rossi." I swallow as Dante checks his pulse again before he swears, nodding at me.

We have unfinished business, you and I.

I push down.

Again.

Again.

Again.

As soon as I hit thirty compressions, Dante leans down and seals his mouth over Dom's, forcing air into his lungs. But there's no rise and fall as we watch his chest.

"Again," I snap, starting a second round. Luciano bends down, and I stare as he forces something into his mouth, pulling his chin up and massaging his neck. He looks up at me.

"Activated charcoal. It might stop the poison from being absorbed into his body."

Poison. Because he always eats my fucking food, *testing* it, despite me telling him not to. I always thought it was overkill.

The tears drop onto his chest.

"Please," I pray. "Please."

"There's a car outside, if we can move him." Vincent is talking, but it sounds garbled as I stare down at Domenico. Dante pinches his nose again, leans down, and it strikes me how strange it is to see him working like that on Dom, fighting to save him, when a few months ago he might have stood back and watched him die without much thought at all.

"Come on, you fucker," he growls down at him as he sits up. "You're too damn pig-headed to go out like this, Rossi."

My hand is trembling over his chest, and it takes me a second to feel it.

The faintest movement beneath my fingers, pushing them up.

And then down again.

"He's breathing – his chest is moving."

I can barely get the words out, but Dante pushes his fingers up against Dom's neck, waiting, before he barks out a low laugh. "I knew it, stubborn asshole. There's a pulse."

Vincent and Tony lift him onto one of the stretchers we keep in the medical bay for emergencies as I stand back, carrying him out of the hall towards the car. "Drive fast."

"You're not coming?" Vincent turns to look at me, everyone turns to look at me.

"Later." My voice is glacial, frost gathering even as the tears still dampen my skin. "I have work to do."

I follow them to the doors, watching as Dom is carefully lifted into the car.

And then I pull the double doors closed, sealing off the room.

Turning, I beckon, and several Crows step forward. "Nobody goes in or out of this room until I am done."

Because someone here is responsible for the terror still radiating through my body, for the horror of watching Domenico gasp and flail for breath.

I intend to find them.

Slowly, I move through the scattered crowd. People turn to watch me with solemn, fearful faces, arms crossed. They murmur to the person next to them, shift on their feet, look towards the door.

People who have nothing to hide.

I know my own suspicions, and they lead me directly to where Leo is seated, a group of men around him all smirking at me. His lip curls as he meets my eye. "Don't look at me. The order was given and obeyed."

"By you, perhaps. But it seems that somebody here missed the memo."

A small crease appears between his eyes, and he glances down the table. Following my own gaze.

Body language is an interesting thing. There are a hundred different ways to give yourself away without ever even opening your mouth.

Most people would assume it's movement. That somebody with something to hide would look shifty, would be shuffling with nerves, eyes glancing everywhere. Guilty.

But here, in this room, it's their stillness that catches my eye. In a space full of nervous people, they hold themselves perfectly, unnaturally still. Eyes down.

By trying not to draw my attention, they have done exactly that.

The crowd whispers as I turn, strolling down the Asante table.

And past it.

When I finally pause, a ripple of whispers echoes behind me.

Paul Maranzano pales. "It wasn't me. I swear it—,"

He flinches as I pat his shoulder. "I know."

And my hand snaps out to grip the throat of the Crow standing beside him. Instinct has Nicolo raising his hands to mine, jagged nails digging into my skin as he tries to pry my grip away.

"Search him."

Paul steps forward, gripping Nicolo's arms as I stand back and let Danny through. I can see the disbelief as he begins to search one of my most senior men, one who has been with me since my first year here. Who has stood by my side, protected me, advised me, laughed with me.

And I see the devastation in Danny's face as he holds up a packet with shaking fingers, even as the same pulses in my own chest.

Nicolo stares at me, his eyes dark. He says nothing. Nothing to argue the contents of the packet that Danny hands me carefully. Nothing to defend himself.

His silence tells me everything I need to know.

And we both know what needs to happen now.

But not before I understand *why*.

"Tell me." The words are harsh, as harsh as the pain raking my insides. Anton Maranzano was one thing. But he wasn't part of my inner circle, wasn't trusted in the way that Nicolo Barbieri has been, close to my side all this time.

For a moment, I wonder if he'll say anything at all.

He nods at me. "The Hawk sends his regards."

It happens in an instant. Nicolo's eyes roll back in his head, legs crumpling. Paul grunts as he tries to catch him, Danny jumping back in shock as Nicolo's legs and arms begin to jerk in a seizure. Foam gathers at the edges of his mouth as he convulses, his body falling still seconds later.

Danny goes to his knees, his hands hovering over Nicolo's body. "Shit, Nic. What the fuck did you do?"

When he looks up at me, my face is empty. "Burn him. He will receive no Call."

I glance around, taking in the ashen faces of those around me. Of my Crows. They look back at me, and all I see is anger at the man who lies dead at my feet.

But I can't help wondering who might be next to try and plunge a knife into my back.

CATERINA

The Hawk.

I try to think as I make my way to my Corvette. It's not a name I'm familiar with. The Corvos have many enemies, but none that have ever made such an obvious assassination attempt.

I pause as I unlock the car. The figure uncurls himself from where he leans against it. "Dante."

"Any news?"

"He's stable. I'm leaving now to head over." Vincent has been keeping me informed, blowing up my phone with updates. But it's not the same as being there, watching the rise and fall of his chest and trying to clear my head of how it felt when it didn't move at all.

He nods. "I thought I might come. We could take my car."

I observe him for a few seconds. "Worried about your muddie?"

He scowls. "That's a fucking awful nickname. And no. He's too fucking stubborn to die so easily. But... I'm worried about you."

I click my tongue. "No need to waste your concern on me. I'm fine."

"Cat." He bars my way as I try to move around him. "Fucking hell. Is it so bad that I'm concerned about you? That I might *care*?"

I open my mouth, but he cuts me off. "Don't give me that political bullshit again. Maybe we're bound by our families' choices, but *we* are the ones who will lead. Not them. And when we are, it's nobody else's business but ours who we choose to love."

I flinch, and he sees it. Sees the weakness I try to hide. Pounces on it. "You don't love me, Dante. You're mistaking lust for love."

His eyes burn as he moves into me until our bodies are pressed together. "Believe me," he breathes. "That is impossible. Because you make it so damn fucking *difficult* to love you, Caterina Corvo, that I couldn't possibly mistake it for anything else."

Our mouths brush, just barely.

"So fucking difficult," he whispers against my lips. "But so fucking easy, too."

There is no thunderbolt clap, no lightning bolt. His lips do not crash into mine. We have always been fire and lightning, he and I – as though putting us together is akin to lighting a match and stepping back to watch us burn.

Not this time.

His hands rise up to cradle my face, his lips sinking into mine as though he's found his fucking home, tasting me softly with a reverence that makes the air catch in my throat, as though he owns my oxygen, controls the breath in my lungs.

He captures the soft moan as it escapes, captures it and breathes it in, his mouth nudging at mine as my lips open and his tongue traces the seam, tasting. As though this is the first time, and we have no history of anger between us.

He kisses me like I hold all of his hopes and dreams in my hand, and when he pulls back, his eyes widen at the look on my face. As his finger reaches out to capture a tear. "*Tentazione*. Why are you crying, *amore*?"

My whole body hurts, but my mouth refuses to say the four words. The words that would undoubtedly condemn me in his eyes.

He would never forgive me.

And I will never forgive myself.

Even as I brace myself to lie to him once again. "It's been a long day. We... we should go. You can drive."

His face drops in concern, his hand stroking across my cheek as I close my eyes and let it happen, even as I despise myself. As I hold his hand in place with my own for a second, drinking in his touch. Stealing a single, precious moment more before I pull his hand back and press a soft kiss to the pulse in his wrist.

And then I drop the keys into his hand, clearing my throat of memories and regret. "Drive carefully, V'Arezzo. I like my car."

Dante

I watch her closely from where I'm leaning against the bland gray wall of the hospital room.

Mainly, I watch the way she watches him. It's as though nobody else exists for her in this moment, only Domenico Rossi. Her hand squeezes his, time and time again, as it lies limp in her grasp.

He will survive. I made damn sure of it. I wasn't going to stop until that asshole's heart was beating again.

Perhaps it would have been easier, to not try quite as hard. Nobody would have expected anything else. I could feel Rocco's stare on my back, feel the questioning glances from my own men as I bent over the Corvo enforcer, forcing the fucking air back into his lungs over and over again until they could do it by themselves.

It would have been one less piece of competition. One less battle for her heart.

But she would never have been the same.

I knew it, instinctively, saw it in the way she curled herself over him, the way she broke in front of everybody. Caterina Corvo never lets herself break, refuses to let the cracks show, but for him, for *him*, she would have snapped, there and then, if I had let him slip away.

And that, I will not allow.

I want her whole. Whole and unbroken, vibrant and passionate, the Caterina who throws punches and passion as easily as she melts in my arms. And she would never have been that Caterina again, without him.

Which poses another question. One I keep turning over and over in my head, trying to solve.

I have no doubt that she belongs to me. She belongs to me in the same vein that I belong to her. In the way that I have always been hers.

I push away the words of my father. It will not come to that. I will make sure of it, make sure that I am never standing across from her as her enemy. I would drop to my knees and let her slit my throat before I ever raised a weapon to her.

But then, there is Domenico Rossi.

How can she ever be truly mine... when she is so clearly *his*, too?

And then there's the cloud. I felt it, felt it come over her even as she softened for me, her fingers gripping at my hair as though I was the only thing keeping her upright, yielding for my lips the way I need her to yield for me.

Something else is bothering her. Something that darkens her expression when she thinks I'm not looking. It hovered over us even as I drove us to the hospital, even as she let me curl my fingers over hers and keep them entwined on my knee. Her face turned towards the window, exhausted and a little lost.

I meant what I said to her. It's a difficult game, loving Caterina.

But nothing worth having ever came easy.

She leans her forehead against his hand, whispering words I can't catch as I turn away to give her some semblance of privacy, checking my phone.

I work through the messages from Rocco, the clipped response to my directions that tells me he's not best pleased with me. I haven't been as focused as I should have been in recent days, but with *il bacio della morte* lifted from Cat's head, it's an issue I can easily resolve.

As I flick through my notifications, my attention snags on an email, sitting unread in my inbox. Scanning it, I feel my brows draw down, even as my eyes move to Caterina. I read it again, taking it in, and then open a blank message. My fingers fly across the screen, my words brief but enough.

I'm taking you up on your offer.

Because despite the removal of Fusco's death sentence, I can still feel the danger in the air. The update I've just read only hardens those suspicions, solidifies them into a knowing.

And it's all focused around her.

My phone vibrates, and I glance at his response.

I'll be ready.

I will allow nothing to happen to Caterina on my watch. Even if that means temporarily allying with Luciano Morelli to make sure.

CATERINA

Warm fingers tangle in my hair. "Caterina."

Awareness is slow. Blearily, I raise my head, blinking to clear my vision, taking in my surroundings.

"Cat."

There's a cough, dry and hacking, and my head shoots up. Domenico is watching me, his gray eyes underscored with dark purple circles. Alive. "You look like shit."

He closes his eyes as a gruff laugh escapes him. "You try being poisoned."

Poisoned. Because of me.

His eyes open again, and he turns his fingers over where I hold his hand, interlacing them with mine. "Turn off that trail of thought."

I stare down at our entwined hands.

"Dom," I whisper. "I thought…"

"Give me some credit." He half-smiles. "I'm made of stronger stuff than that."

Blowing out a breath, I let my head sink into his side, breathing him in above the sharp, bleached medical scent. He's still here. "You're not allowed to taste my food anymore. I forbid it."

He squeezes my hand in gentle rebuke. "That's my job, Cat. If I hadn't, then it would be you in this bed. If you survived at all."

His voice is a little stronger, and the grim tone has me shaking my head. "So it's alright for you to be here, but not for me."

"That sounds about right." He tries to shift, to pull himself up before he collapses back with a groan. "Jesus. Help me up."

"Why?" Carefully, I slide my arm around his shoulders. A pained wheeze escapes him as he curls his hands into the bars.

"I'm discharging myself."

I drop him. Half in surprise, but also half in sheer fucking irritation, because Domenico Rossi is easily the most bull-headed man I have ever met.

And that really is saying something, considering my upbringing. "You are *not* discharging yourself!"

He gives me a long-suffering look. "You're not going back there without me. I forbid it."

Make that one hundred fucking per cent irritation. He grunts as I punch him in the arm. "Fucking hell, Cat. I'm in *hospital,* woman. Have pity on me."

Crossing my arms, I glare at him. "You can't have it both ways, Domenico. And what the hell do you mean, you *forbid* it?"

"Someone tried to poison you. I need to find out who."

He continues to try to pull himself up, failing every time. Meanwhile, I stand there, tapping my feet on the floor and debating whether I should just knock him out.

He would get more rest. I would feel much better.

Feels like a win-win.

When he finally sinks back down, his chest heaving, I walk over and poke him in the chest. "You done?"

He grimaces, squeezing his eyes shut. "I'll try again in a minute."

I take a deep breath. A deep, deep breath. And then another one, praying for patience. "If you're done with your little pseudo-Superman routine, I could always explain that I already *know* who did it, because I'm not completely useless, and you could listen. Instead of charging off half-cocked, even though you *were dead a few damn hours ago*."

"Cat—," his voice is placating, but I'm not having any of it.

"You died, Dom," I snap hoarsely. "You died in front of me. You stopped fucking *breathing*, and if it wasn't for Dante, I doubt you'd be sitting here griping at me now, and all you can think about is going back for *round fucking two*?"

I stop, my breath heaving in harsh pants, and glare at him.

Waiting.

He presses his lips together. "Don't ask me to apologize for keeping you safe, Cat. I'll be spending the rest of my life on my knees if that's the case."

God, he's such a stubborn shit. "I don't need a protector, Dom, I just need—,"

You. I just need you.

The harsh line of his jaw softens. "Come here, Caterina."

I tip my chin up. "I'm not helping you get out of here. You're staying until the doctor discharges you."

He rolls his eyes at me, rumpled and exhausted, but still here. "I *said*, come here, Caterina."

I don't know when our relationship slipped into this. From enforcer and boss to something... more.

Silently, I pad across the room. He lifts his arm, shifting himself to the side as I slide in beside him. Lay my head on his shoulder. I feel his breath across my hair, my heart faintly stuttering as he presses his lips against my head.

Still here with me.

And finally, I can breathe.

***

I exit the room, a sleeping Domenico behind me, and glance up and down.

Dante unfolds himself from one of the plastic chairs dotted around. "How is he?"

"Alive. Thanks to you."

His lips tilt up. "I have the feeling that he would have survived without my help."

Maybe, but I won't forget it anytime soon. "We can't stay much longer. I need to get back."

I can't forget the chaos I left behind me. A dead soldier – a *traitor* – and I have no idea why. I sent Vincent and Tony back when I arrived to help Danny with clean-up, Vincent in particular needed to support the younger intake, but I have my own responsibilities to fulfill.

"I'm ready when you are." Then he hesitates. "Have you seen the message?"

I frown. "What message?"

"From our esteemed leaders." His tone is faintly mocking as he retrieves his phone from his pocket, flicking through and handing it to me. I read through swiftly, confusion filling me. "A campus social? Why?"

He shrugs. "Apparently, to foster better relations among the Cosa Nostra. Not like it's the first time."

Maybe not, but the timing couldn't be any fucking worse. Although, with the *il bacio della morte* removed, at least I have a chance at surviving it. "Wonderful. Can't wait."

As we're leaving, my own phone goes off. Pausing, I dig around, finally locating it in my back pocket. My heart sinks when I see the name. "Sorry. I need to take this."

"I'll wait in the car." He walks away from me as I slide my finger across the screen.

My voice is strained. "Papa."

"Carissimo." His voice is clipped. It seems to be that way more often than not at the moment. The social calls seem to have stopped altogether, everything purely business. "Did you see the message?"

"About the social?" I take a seat on the wooden bench outside the main hospital doors, glancing around. "I did. It sounds delightful."

Truthfully, I'd rather have my nails pulled out one by one, but I doubt he'd appreciate hearing that.

"Excellent. I'll be there the following day. All of us will."

I straighten. "That is... unexpected. May I ask why?"

My father grunts. "You can, but all in good time, *carissimo*. I assume the Fusco girl is taken care of?"

"Giovanni Fusco has been managed. *Il bacio della morte* has been lifted."

Silence. It goes on for so long that I pull the phone away to check the connection in case it's dropped.

"Caterina," he says finally. "That is not what I ordered."

Ice. That's what washes over me at that moment. "You wanted him managed—,"

"I wanted him *broken*," he snaps. "I ordered you to use the sister. Managed is *not good enough*."

My hands begin to shake. Abruptly, I stand, turning one way and then the other, my feet eating up the distance as I pace. "Papa, this is not necessary. We have agreed—,"

"*I do not care what is necessary!*" His roar echoes down the call, so much that I have to yank it away from my ear. "I gave you a fucking order, Caterina. I expect it to be followed."

It feels as though the ground has been ripped out from under my feet.

I had it handled. It was *done*.

But it's not enough for my father.

He wants blood. Rosa Fusco's blood, and he will not settle for anything less.

"You have until I arrive," he says in a low tone. "Matteo will be attending with me. And if you cannot do what needs to be done, Caterina, then I am certain he will be only too happy to carry out the orders of his *capo*."

My eyes squeeze closed. I take a breath, trying to think, trying to come up with anything, anything to push away the decision he leaves me with.

"It is not only your position at stake," he says softly. "Perhaps you should remember that, daughter. I have been very understanding, considering your actions of late. But my patience is running thin."

And just like that, any glimpse of hope is brutally stamped out.

I don't know what to say to this man. I barely recognise him. The words collect in my throat. Begging, pleading.

But he hangs up, without waiting for me to say a single thing.

Caterina

I blink as Dante opens the car door. He holds out a hand, his green eyes examining me.

I didn't even realize we were back. Too lost in my own head, trying to find a way to save Rosa Fusco. To stop her from meeting the same end as Nicoletta.

And I have failed.

I accept his hand gingerly, dropping it as soon as I'm out. "Thanks for the ride. I... I'm going to head in. It's late."

"Tell me." His voice is low. "Whatever the matter is, *tentazione*. I can help."

Temptation. It has never felt so appropriate. I could unload this onto him. His shoulders are broad enough to help me carry the load.

But he won't be able to fix this, any more than I can. Less so, from his position as a V'Arezzo. It would only put him in the middle of something none of us can possibly win.

And I have no wish to ask him to bear witness to what I'm about to do.

So I shake my head, turning my back on him. "It's been a long day, that's all. You don't need to stay this evening."

It's been a long year. Endless.

But nothing has felt so hard as this.

Even my apartment feels wrong as I let myself in, slowly pushing the door shut behind me. Domenico isn't lingering, making coffee, making a damn nuisance of himself, and I feel his absence like the loss of a limb.

But he isn't here, and I wouldn't put this on him either. I know precisely what he would say. What he would choose. And at this moment, I'm glad that he isn't here. Glad that he's away from this, from watching me shred the person I thought I was – that I know *he* thinks I am – into bloody ribbons.

My eyes fall on the cream envelope propped up against the counter. It feels heavy in my hands, and as I shake the key into my hand, a slip of paper falls out.

Directions.

My eyes lift, taking in the emptiness of my apartment. And I turn, the door closing behind me as I stride out, Luc's directions clutched in my hand.

***

I would never have found it without them. I doubt anybody ever would.

I circle the small, square, white-walled building in fascination. Set between an entwined pair of oak trees in the middle of the woods bordering campus, to get to it I had to almost crawl through, until it opened up into a passageway.

Whoever built this place clearly didn't want to be found or disturbed. A single window is set into the angled roof, none in the four walls. Privacy, indeed.

The oiled door swings open without complaint, and I step inside. The air feels warm, and I wonder if Luciano has been here today. A lamp has been left on in the corner, next to a small bed with a carved wooden headboard pushed against the plain wall, neatly made up with soft looking blankets. The tiny kitchenette looks like it holds coffee and not much else, and a tiny television in the corner is framed with stacks of books, facing a battered-looking leather armchair. A handwoven rug against buttery-colored wooden floors finishes the overall look.

I blink. It's... cozy. Not what I would have expected, from Luciano Morelli.

But it's exactly what I need. Space to think.

It takes a moment to toe off my heeled boots, flexing the ache from my toes as I cross the floor to the bed. Fingers trailing against the soft, fleeced green blanket, I decide to take Luc at his word and grasp it, wrapping it around my shoulders and sitting down on the edge.

Carefully, I lay down, pressing my cheek against the soft pillow that smells faintly of Luciano, mint and familiar musky sandalwood, like the aftershave he always wears. Has always worn, for as long as I've known him.

I take a deep breath, and then another.

Luciano

I pause in the doorway, not expecting her to be there.

Her chest rises and falls in soft huffs, her eyes closed. She doesn't stir when I nudge the door closed, as my feet cross the room. Not wanting to scare her, I take a seat down by her feet, the bed dipping under my weight.

And I watch her. Just for a moment. Just to soak in the sight of her like this, vulnerable and soft, a Caterina I haven't seen for a long time. She's always so full of life that seeing her in this way feels like an intimacy I haven't earned.

I don't want to wake her, but I have a feeling she won't appreciate my presence. So I stand up, meaning to leave her in peace, but a quiet voice stills me.

"Luc?"

I glance down, taking in her wide brown eyes, the loose braid with hints of bronze curls springing free. "I didn't realize you were here. Stay as long as you need to. I'm heading out now."

But she's shaking her head, sitting up and swinging her legs out. "I didn't mean to fall asleep – I have to go. What time is it?"

I check my watch. "Just after twelve."

The witching hour. She slows, blowing out a breath of relief. "Oh. Good. That's... good."

I notice her fingers trembling. She follows my gaze, curls them inward. "I'll be out of your way now."

"No rush." Instead, I sit down next to her. "Want to talk about it?"

I'm not expecting an answer at all. Maybe a sarcastic comment, some sort of brush off. But she doesn't give me either of those things.

"What do you see when you look in the mirror, Luc?"

Her question takes me by surprise. When I look down, she's staring at the wall across from us. So I bite back the flippant response, taking a minute or two to think it through.

"I see... many things. Some are things that I like, and there are some that I don't. But I face them all the same. Who are we after all, if not the consequences of our own decisions?"

She nods beside me, slowly. "I wonder if that will happen to us all, in the end. If over time, that balance tips. Until in the end we stop looking in the mirror at all, because there is so much about ourselves that we can't bear to see."

"I draw the lines that I will not cross," I say quietly. "I hope that means that in the years to come, I will still see someone to be proud of. That my children will be proud of."

She stiffens. "What if you needed to cross that line?"

I loosen my breath. "Then I would ask myself whether the reward was worth the sacrifice. I'm not so idealistic as to believe that time will never come. Not in our world. There will always be a line to cross, little crow. And we will always need to make a choice about whether or not to cross it. That is a burden we all have to bear."

I watch her from the corner of my eye as she contemplates my response. And I wonder what her lines are, and what it would cost her to cross them.

But before I can ask, she stands up. "Thank you. This place is... I like it."

"Good." I half-smile. "Come back anytime."

She only nods, her gaze distant.

And then she's gone, as if she was never here at all.

CATERINA

I know what I have to do.

I know what my line is, and what it will take for me to cross it. What the cost will be.

But even as I sit, alone at the dais the next morning, I still battle with the weight of my decision. The Crows cast glances at me from our table, at the empty plate in front of me. It's Vincent who approaches me in the end. It takes a moment for me to pull my eyes away from my careful watch over one particular table, to slide them towards him. "Yes?"

He hesitates, and I don't blame him. I needed every piece of armor this morning, took my time building up the image of Caterina Corvo, ready to present to the world. The Corvo heir is here, displayed in the heaviness of my make-up, the straight, sleek ponytail of my straightened hair high on my head. In my vibrant, scarlet blazer, matching my heels. My knives and guns are on full display.

I am dressed for war, and they can read the signs.

"Do you want me to get you something? With Dom out, I mean."

"No," I say softly. "Thank you. I'm not hungry this morning, Vincent."

He waits. "Are you... sure?"

He is not asking about food.

My eyes follow Rosa Fusco, tracking her movements as she smiles at Leo, acknowledging his look of concern. She answers his question, before he turns to speak to some of the Fusco men. As she cradles her coffee, her arms tucked in tightly, her face wreathed in shadows when nobody else is looking.

This is the line.

I watch as she casts a glance down the table, quietly sliding out of her seat. Leaving the dining hall, with her hands tucked under her arms. Alone.

And I make the decision.

"Go," I say quietly. "Now, Vincent."

He nods, once.

And then he's gone.

And as I sit there, the nausea clawing up my throat, I pray that the cost will be worth it. That it won't be everything that has ever mattered to me.

***

It does not take long.

By lunchtime, the entire campus is buzzing with gossip. People turn to look at me as I make my way back towards the dining hall. At what I hold in my hand.

He reaches me before I even open the doors.

Hands wrench me back, and then he slams me against the door, so hard that I taste the iron of my own blood in my mouth. A cold hand grips my throat. "Where is she?"

When I don't answer, he smacks my head back against the door again until I see stars instead of the gray skies above. "Where the *fuck* is she?"

There's a ruckus, and my neck is released, the air rushing back into my throat as I cough. I straighten, massaging the skin, and Giovanni shouts with fury as they hold him back.

Luciano. Dante. Both of them here, cursing, fighting to stop Gio from going for my throat again.

"The *fuck*, Fusco?"

Dante looks between Gio and I. "Cat – what the hell is going on?"

"*Where is my fucking sister?*"

Giovanni Fusco does not shout. He *screams* it, screams as if his voice could reach the heavens.

I can already tell by the devastated look on his face that my father will get his wish.

I want him broken.

I am, after all, my father's daughter. A Corvo.

And so, I break him.

Casually, I fling the bundle in my hand to the floor, watching as it scatters.

The thick, auburn strands dance on the wind, catching on Giovanni's shoes. Viscous, sticky dark blood sticks to the leather. Luc and Dante drop their grip and he slowly reaches down, gathering the reddish strands up in his hands. Cupping them gently. Rubbing his sister's blood between his fingers.

I don't want to look.

Don't want to look at him as he sinks to his knees.

Don't want to look at Dante, at the comprehension there, the dawning horror.

At Luciano's face, as he realizes what my line was.

Hands grip my face, digging in.

"Tell me you didn't," Dante breathes, and my throat burns at the raw desperation in his voice. "You wouldn't do that, Cat. You *wouldn't*. Tell me it's not true."

My eyes meet Luc's over his shoulder, and I have to close them. "I did what I had to. It's done."

And Dante freezes. His hands slowly, so slowly, lower from my face. His green eyes stare into mine as if searching for the truth.

As if he sees the lies.

When he takes a step away from me, it *hurts*.

But I knew what the cost would be. So I keep my chin up, even as he backs away, shaking his head. Even as my heart threatens to rip directly from my chest, as he moves to Gio. Kneeling beside him, whispering something to him that I cannot hear. His hand on his shoulder as he tries to lift him, to shield him from the eyes gathering around us.

Luc is still watching me, his face grave. "Was the cost worth the consequences?"

I meet his gaze.

"I don't know yet."

CATERINA

I reject the call from Domenico.

The first.

The fifth.

At some point, I lose count. That's when I turn my phone off.

Vincent knocks on the door, his phone in his hand.

"Tell him I'm busy." My voice is short.

There is a line of Crows outside, spread across the clearing, dotted between the trees. Ready and waiting.

I check the time. The social will be starting soon, although I'm not expecting to attend. But as the minutes pass, it becomes clear that nobody is coming.

Slowly, I strip out of my layers. I carefully redo my makeup with a steady hand, let my hair down before sweeping it up into an intricate knot. Ready for another show.

At this point, I don't know how many I have left in me.

But at least I look the part. My dress plunges to the floor, the deep v-shaped neckline dipping almost to my stomach, held in place by a corset design with silk black laces curving up my back. From my hips, it sweeps out to the floor, the train a good foot long.

Layer upon layer of iridescent color. Shimmering black feathers, intermixed with deep, deep purple and the darkest indigo to create a sleek waterfall that falls in graceful waves.

It's a dress that draws the eye.

But I turn away from my own reflection.

My hands struggle to pull the laces at the back tightly enough for the front to stay in place, and I mentally resign myself to asking Vincent for help. I pull open the door without thinking, reliant on my Crows outside, and my eyes fall on a pair of black shoes.

Dante pushes inside, closing the door behind us. "Cat."

My throat feels dry, and I cross to the sink. "They shouldn't have let you up."

Dante's hands land on my shoulders. "Nobody keeps me from you. Tell me the damned truth, Cat. I know you. I know you better than you know yourself, and I know for a fucking fact that you wouldn't hurt Rosa Fusco. So where is she?"

For a moment, I can't breathe. He has so much faith in me.

So much more faith than I have in myself.

Instead of answering, I turn, my voice harsh. "Since you're here, you can do me up."

He yanks on the laces to the point of pain, tying them deftly before he turns me. "For the love of God, Caterina. *Listen to me*, damn you. This is serious. They will kill you for this. Whatever plan you have, it doesn't matter."

"They've been trying for a while now. This is nothing new."

"Gio has nothing left to *lose*. He's a shattered man."

"That was the point." I can't quite hold onto my tone, the volume dropping. "I will meet whatever comes. You see what you want to see, Dante. You always have."

"I don't believe you," he breathes. "You won't even speak to Dom. Why?"

I breathe. Breathe in, breathe out. "Because he will not agree with what I have done."

Truth.

The seeds of doubt begin to show on his face. "You're lying."

Shaking my head, I move to the door. "I'm sorry that I am not who you want me to be, Dante. I did what needed to be done. It was either me, or it would have been Matteo. I spared her that, at least. It's the only thing I was able to give."

A dignified death. Not a terror-soaked, drawn-out dismemberment. Fear and pain and violation.

All any of us can ask for in the end. I wonder if I will receive the same.

I hide my shaking hands in my gown. "I need to leave now."

"Don't go." Dante pauses, and I hate him for trying, one more time. Almost as much as I love him for it. "Don't go, Cat. Leave now, while you can. Get back to your father's estate where you'll be safe. Please."

If there is one thing I have learned, it is that running to my father is not the safest option.

Smiling a little, I reach up and brush a little mark away from his tuxedo. He looks flawless, sharp and dangerous in black. "Goodbye, Dante."

And then I sweep out, leaving him framed in my doorway.

I'm not worried about the locks. I doubt I'll be coming back.

Caterina

I haven't set foot in the main hall for months. Certainly not since I came back.

The pulsing bass of music greets us as I walk up the steps, Vincent and Danny on either side of me. They don't speak to me, as they haven't since I walked out of my apartment and left Dante V'Arezzo behind.

I can feel their judgment. Feel it from the others, too. The censure. Paul Maranzano looked as though he might spit on me as I passed him.

They don't understand. And they won't, not until they face a similar choice, have to face crossing their own lines. We all have them.

I nod towards the doors. "Open them."

The men around me stir, exchanging glances over my head.

"I said, *open the doors*." At my snap, they slowly move ahead.

The main hall is far more ornate than the dining hall. This is the place where we gather for formal occasions, though none have ever felt so somber as this one. The atmosphere is chilled as we walk through. This is no party.

The only light comes from the golden chandeliers above our heads. Each one is lit with dozens of slim candles, casting flickering light and shadows across the floor. At the bar, smartly dressed staff in black offer every possible choice, from the best champagne to the finest brandy.

The dons have not skimped on the expenses for tonight.

Everywhere I look, people are drinking. Most of them heavily. A few of the more inebriated stumble into our path, quickly pushed back by my guards, as I push on, the train of my dress flowing out behind me.

Towards the thrones set up in the middle of the room.

How fucking ludicrous. One for each of us, as if we're gods. As though we're not just as flawed and human as the rest of them.

Stefano is the only other heir present. He watches as I ascend the small steps, sweeping my skirts around. Settling into the middle throne, I grip the gilded edges. The intricate gold decoration cuts sharply into the back of my legs through the feathers of my gown.

"Evening, Stefano."

"You should not be here." His voice is just loud enough to hear over the music.

I don't turn my head. "I am exactly where I need to be."

In a place where I can watch. Noting the people in attendance. Asantes, Morellis and V'Arezzos mingle in small groups, loiter at the bar. *Mingle*, as directed by the dons.

The next generation of the Cosa Nostra. There will be fighting tonight, or fucking.

Probably both.

I don't see a single Fusco.

Even the Crows are thin on the ground, the bulk made up by the men who spread out in a line in front of the five thrones. I spot Amie, pretty and perfect in a bright gold gown, but she turns away rather than meet my eyes.

Breathe in. Breathe out.

I show no discomfort as I sit there, watching. Stefano joins the rest of the Asantes, but I remain where I am, my back straight.

Alone.

And as the evening crawls along, I wait.

Because they are coming.

I glimpse Dante and Luciano in the crowd below, working their way through. They don't turn towards me – don't look my way at all, it seems.

So I sit there, waiting. Trying not to think about Dante. Luciano. Or about Domenico, who will be raging in his hospital bed as nobody picks up the phone.

But above all, I try not to think about Rosa and Giovanni Fusco.

The crowd grows steadily more active as the night passes. Quiet, serious conversation turns to drunken calls and shouts, the noise growing into an almost deafening buzz that rises above the music. Someone falls over in their drunken stupor, taking a table with him. Glasses smash to the floor, red wine soaking into the pristine white tablecloth.

A moving, pulsing wave of animals.

And then a frenzy erupts.

Luciano

The smoke fills the room quickly, obscuring my view.

People start to scream, the crowd pushing wildly around me. Pushing me back, forcing me to turn from where I want to be. The noxious, sulphuric scent fills my nose, chokes up my lungs as I try to bellow at the men ahead. "Get those fucking doors open!"

Nobody is paying attention, everyone fighting.

In front of me, a girl – a V'Arezzo – goes down with a scream, someone climbing straight over her without pausing. Cursing, I reach down and wrap my hand around her arm, dragging her upright as she sobs. But she's not the only one. The crowd clamors at the doors, people pressing in behind them and making it impossible for them to get out.

People are going to die unless we get those doors open. The smoke won't kill anyone, although it might injure, but the crush is the real danger here.

Desperate, I glance behind me, but the thrones are completely hidden from view by the black smog. "*Dante!*"

No response. As if he could hear me over the shouts and screams as people claw to survive.

I fight, trying to get forward whilst pulling people back, but it's a losing battle. Bodies press into me from all sides, and I tilt my head up, trying to take a breath. Getting a lungful of smoke for my trouble.

And all the while, people push behind me. Pushing forward.

Desperate, I start to push sideways instead. Across, instead of forward. It's a fucking slog as people claw to get ahead, but my hands touch the wall, the bodies opening up to a small pocket of empty space as I drop down and take a deep breath where the air is clearer.

I edge my way down the room, my hands feeling along the walls as I go. Searching. Smoke still obscures my view of Caterina's seat, but pockets are opening up, the smoke drifting away and leaving hazy wisps in their wake.

I close my eyes in brief relief as my hand meets something metallic. The fucking fire escape.

It resists, but I shove it hard, and it opens with a screech. Cold, fresh air floods in, and I take a breath, pushing open the other door and ducking back inside.

"That way!" I grab anyone I can, almost throwing them in the direction of the exit until the crowd starts to turn. To move towards fresh air.

A few crumpled bodies remain where they are, and I dart between them, checking each pulse. Everyone is still breathing.

"Luc!" A bellow, and I glance up, sagging at Nico's relieved expression. He grips me tightly in a brief embrace, his hand clapping against my shoulder. "Fucking hell. What the fuck was that?"

"Here." Hauling the unconscious Asante at my feet into my arms, I pass her to Nic. "Get everyone out. I need to find Cat, Nic."

Because this wasn't a fucking accident.

No, it was a distraction.

When I reach the thrones, Dante is already there.

Staring at Cat's empty seat, his body frozen.

Grabbing his shoulders, I shake him. "Could she have gotten out?"

He looks grim. "No."

I look behind the thrones. "There."

We burst through the door into an old hallway. Dante is ahead of me as he sprints ahead, to the very end. Where a set of doors are ajar, banging slightly in the breeze.

His face is ashen as he picks something up from the floor. "Luc."

The feather glints in his hand.

"We split up." I push him through, out into the mud, trees and trails leading to fuck knows where branching off in every direction. "They could be anywhere."

"She might already be—,"

"She's not," I snap. My hand drops, making sure my guns are still in place. "They'll make a spectacle of it, whatever it is. We just need to get to her first. They won't be far."

They have a few minutes' head start. That's all.

As long as we follow the right trail.

Caterina

Awareness returns in a blinding, ripping bolt of pain.

I surge upright, the scream locked in my throat as the agony in my shoulder twists violently.

"That's better."

My head swivels to the side as I retch, rolling over. The stink of egg and sulfur lingers in my nose.

Smoke. So much smoke.

And I couldn't get out.

Except the floor beneath me is not marble but cool, packed mud, my fingers digging into it, leaving marks embedded in the ground. Gasping, I lay my cheek against the earth.

The kick hits me somewhere around the left side of my ribcage. My scream is raw as something *cracks*, my body flipping over and rolling to a slumped stop.

Panting, I try to pull myself upright, try to reach for my knives—

"Looking for these?"

I blink, staring upwards as my daggers dangle in front of me. "I was."

Thanks to the smoke, on top of the still healing marks from my recent strangulation attempts, not much comes out.

The man crouches down, and fingers grip my chin. "Hello, Corvo bitch."

Grimacing, I try to pull away, but he holds me easily. "Leo."

Giovanni's enforcer smiles, a twisted, triumphant smirk, eyes glittering with jubilation. And something... darker. "Surprise."

"Not really," I force out. "A little obvious, to be honest."

The blow rocks my head to the side, my ears ringing as pain rips through my cheek, drawing a choked groan from my throat. I reach up, my fingers smearing in wet liquid that drips down my face.

Leo holds up his hand, wiggling his fingers. "I brought it especially for you."

The brass knuckle duster gleams in the light from the stars ahead as he stands. Pushing myself up onto my knees, I bite back the moan at the pain in my ribs.

A circle of Fuscos surrounds me. Every face is staring down at me with revulsion.

There will be no mercy here.

Gathering up the bloody phlegm in my mouth, I spit it onto the ground at Leo's feet. "Stealing ideas from the Crows, Leo? Awfully unimaginative. The circle is *our* thing."

His face twists into fury. "You dare. Dare to make fucking *jokes*, while Rosa's body isn't even cold yet. Where is she?"

When I stay silent, he grabs my head, twisting it. "See that? That's where you're going, Crow. Tell us where she is, and I'll shoot you before I put you in."

My pulse begins to race, my heart jumping in painful leaps as I look at the site of my execution.

The wooden box is small. Enough that I know I won't fit properly. They'll have to force my legs up, twist them. Break them, maybe. The hole next to it is obvious enough.

Sweat beads up along my hairline, sliding down to mix with the blood on my face. "Probably not my preferred option, truth be told."

He leans into my face, spit flecking across my skin as he bellows. "Tell me where she is!"

I brace myself. But I say nothing.

The kick is harder this time, directly into my abdomen, and my head smacks against something hard as I crash into the ground, the air rushing out of me as I gasp for breath. "A-animals."

He pauses. "Say that again."

"Animals," I gasp. "I... got rid of it. The evidence."

His face nearly crumples. "She wasn't *evidence*. She was a person. Like Nicci was a fucking person, you fucking cunt."

Brace.

Breathe.

He grabs my hair, twisting it around his fists. "I'm almost glad you won't tell us. You deserve nothing but a slow death, Corvo."

And he begins to pull. It feels like my scalp will rip from my head as my feet scrabble, trying to keep up. As he drags me towards my own grave.

I fight, then, fight as best I can, but my body is as weak as a fucking newborn kitten. My head is ringing, my shoulder burning, pain ripping through my body, but I scratch and claw and punch, until Leo grabs my face in his hand and smashes his fist into it.

The crunch of my nose breaking under his hand is audible. Much louder than my cry, broken and rasping and weak.

I can't fight them all. Not half-blind and filled with pain.

And the fear. The fear is crawling up my throat, sealing off my ability to breathe.

We are all born expecting to die. We live the reality of it every day. Knowing that at some point, a knife will find its mark. The gun will meet its target.

But nobody expects to die like this.

They slowly force me down into the box, pushing and twisting until I can't hold back my scream at the agony in my legs. They don't fit, just as I thought, and I grunt as someone holds me down for Leo to tie them into place, forcing them into an angle that they'd never normally contort into.

He's out of breath when he stands. I stare blankly at the edges of the cheap pine, at the whorls in the wood. And then I turn my head, looking up at the sky. Drinking in the sight of the stars.

The pain is almost indescribable, my legs already cramping.

They take my wrists next, wrapping the rope around them. The air is full around me, full of wishes for a long and horrific death. Vile taunts ring out, money exchanges hands on how long it will take for my lungs to run out of oxygen. Someone calls out not to scream, because it takes up too much oxygen.

Leo has one final gift for me.

I stare at the bag, and I start to struggle again.

Not that. Please, not that.

"This is goodbye, Caterina Corvo." His voice is almost soft. "If it makes you feel better, this is still a better death than what Nicoletta had."

He ignores my pleading, shoving something that smells strongly like oil into my mouth. "Can't have you removing yourself from the game early, can we?"

I take one final, desperate glimpse at the stars before Leo forces the dark material over my head. Before my world narrows down to the sound of rushing blood in my ears, to the hot feel of my own breath against the cloth.

A dull thud sounds. Another.

And then I'm moving, the box lifted.

I land with a jolt.

I promised myself I wouldn't cry.

I swore it.

And I break that promise, smash it into pieces, as the soft thudding of earth landing on my coffin sounds above me.

I don't want to die in the dark.

The tears come fast, salty and damp as I try to stop myself from breathing too deeply, trying to conserve oxygen. Try not to make any noise in case they hear it, use it to taunt the people I'm leaving behind.

I will never be able to tell Dante the truth.

I will never be able to rest my head against Dom's shoulder again.

I will never sit next to Luc in our secret space and ask him about the daggers.

And I'll never—

No.

I refuse to taint any of those memories.

And as they bury me in the cold, dark earth, I close my eyes. Steady myself.

I am Caterina Corvo. And I will not die screaming.

Instead, I start counting the minutes.

Waiting for it to be over.

Luciano

I push another branch out of the way, snapping it as I force my way through the dense undergrowth. The seconds are ticking too quickly, time slipping away.

There is no noise to help guide me. Nothing aside from the wind in the trees, nothing that will give me an indication of where she might be. Nothing but the whistle of the breeze, the rustle of leaves brushing against each other above my head.

At any other time, it would be soothing. But not now, not with the perspiration building at the back of my neck, the desperation threatening to choke me.

Because if I fail - if Dante fails – if neither of us can find her in these godforsaken fucking woods, she will not survive the night.

The notion is impossible. I will not allow that to happen.

I'm coming, little crow. You just need to hold on until I get there.

My breathing turns rough and jagged, my footsteps sinking into the dirt as my legs break into a run.

Snap.

My head turns, and I stop short. Listening. Ears straining, my eyes scanning the trees on my right.

Another snap. A sound that doesn't belong here,

This sound is human. The shuffle that follows as they try to stay silent only makes it more obvious, and I change direction, carefully making my way off the worn path. Stopping to listen.

More than one set of footsteps walks through these woods. A group.

My gun is a reassuring weight in my hand, and my finger slips onto the trigger. Waiting.

Ready to start a war, if I need to.

But the noises move away from me, fading away into the distance. As if they're returning to the campus.

As if they've finished the job.

When my feet find another trail, I waste no time, darting back in the opposite direction to the noise behind me. I follow the broken twigs, snapped-off branches, and track the depressions left by heavy boots in the mud.

Caterina is close. She has to be.

Except the trail runs cold as I reach a small clearing, the forest returning to its natural state. Slowly, I turn. My eyes rake my surroundings, trying to assess which direction to go in from here.

But there is nothing. Nothing that gives me any fucking indication, any clue.

Dark thoughts threaten to push their way in, even as I fight to force them away.

Because the notion of a world without her in it is impossible.

And unacceptable.

I walk across the clearing, examining every possible angle, every potential route. But there is nothing.

And if she is not beyond this point, then she is *here*. Or she was.

The brightness of the stars above casts a dim light across the ground, and I take a few steps. My eyes turning down, seeing the shape of shoes, the evidence of footsteps moving in every direction. Back and forth, as though they were walking in fucking circles.

Or if they were focused on something. Something on the ground.

Concentrate.

I carefully trace the steps, note where they turn messy and convoluted. Find where they gathered en masse, clustered together. Crouching, I run my finger over the earth.

And then I see it.

So easy to miss, I almost skate right over it.

But there. A boundary line, the footsteps ending abruptly. I turn on the flashlight from my phone, turn it to face the ground.

And when I see the rectangle, the packed, neatly patted down piece of dirt that holds no footsteps, bare of leaves and debris from the forest floor, it takes me precious, wasted fucking moments to understand what I'm seeing.

And clarity hits me. Not like a lightning bolt. But in a dawning, curling horror that wraps around my heart and chokes it, strangles the oxygen from my lungs with creeping, insidious talons.

The phone drops from my hand, bouncing across the floor and clattering to a stop, casting a broken beam of light over the grave in front of me.

A noise that no human should ever make sounds deep in my chest.

No.

My knees hit the ground, and I shove my fingers into the dirt. Grabbing, yanking, clawing, as fast as I can. My hands burn, the nails ripping away as I dig.

But I keep going, tearing away the dirt that keeps her trapped beneath.

And I pray.

Luciano

Time becomes meaningless.

My blood soaks into the mud, my nails left behind as jagged tributes.

There are no measures of time but the piles of dirt building around me. Not fast enough.

I claw, my fingers scrabbling for purchase as I grab it in clumps, throwing it to the side and behind me, trying desperately to get deeper.

Layer upon layer of mud, stones catching my skin, tearing it as I give everything I am to freeing her.

They can have it.

Have every piece of me, every drop of blood in my body.

For her, I give it freely.

Finally, *finally*, my fingers scrape against rough, coarse wood.

The seconds crawl as I rip away the last of the dirt, clearing the edges away until I can grip the edges of the makeshift coffin lid, the planks roughly nailed together. My arms shake, with exertion and adrenaline and soul crushing fear as I yank it away, pulling it up with a grunt and heaving it to the side.

She curls on her side as though sleeping. Rope covers her, rough and coarse, folding her legs up, binding her wrists.

Ice, and heat, and ice again, as I take in the cloth over her head.

Caterina, Caterina, Caterina—

Her name is a silent chant inside my head, the pulsing movement of whatever blood is left inside me, the prayer on my lips as I reach in, careful to keep my balance. My arms slide beneath her so easily; my little, broken crow, in her iridescent gown of feathers.

But she does not move as I lift her out, her limbs limp and dragging along the floor.

Out of habit, I look for the knives to cut her free.

But there are no weapons. They took them from her, separated her from the blades that make up part of who she is, vibrant and warm and so fucking alive, and they put her under the ground, in the cold and the dark.

She feels like air in my arms, as I fold my body over hers, curling myself over her in an attempt to transfer some of my warmth into her cold body.

The rage is a storm, building inside my chest.

I don't want to look, don't want to have the knowledge in my head of what her eyes look like with the essence of her soul stripped away from them. But I won't leave her in the dark.

The moan hovers on my lips as I gently, so fucking gently, tug the strings at the bottom of the bag around her head, lift it up and off, her hair spilling out across my arm. As I see the swollen injuries, the darkened skin as bruises form where somebody took out their anger on her face.

But it catches before it reaches the air, as I look into her eyes.

Caterina Corvo gazes back at me. And as I watch, her eyelids close slowly, and open again.

My voice breaks on the words, relief and fear and anger fighting for dominance. "Little crow."

Her lips part, but no words come out. But her chest rises and falls, the smallest, smallest amount.

And when I press shaking fingers against her neck, her pulse is strong, thumping slowly underneath my touch.

I sit back hard on my ass, keeping her with me, my arms tight around her as I hold her close. "I've got you, Caterina. I've got you."

The words I want to say all wrestle for space inside my mouth, until all I can do is press my lips against her cold hair. "Just breathe. I have you."

And slowly, she closes her eyes, taking a deep breath of the fresh air and turning her head to press her cheek against the warmth of my chest.

She doesn't speak.

But she's here.

Caterina

I focus on breathing.

Slow, steady.

Pushing the air out, and bringing it back in.

Precious, limited air.

Luc's arms are gentle as he carries me. He doesn't speak, doesn't push for more than I can give, and I'm grateful.

I don't have any words in me right now. It's all I can do to keep breathing.

Darkness.

My nails scratching against the wood.

The thud, thud, thud, of the dirt hitting me from above.

I am still there. I don't trust this, don't trust that it's not something dreamed up inside my head, some disassociation from the terror of being trapped in a box as the air slowly drains away.

But my fingers, cold and numb, curl around the inner edge of his shirt, holding on to his warmth, brushing the skin underneath. Until

I am certain that this version of Luciano Morelli doesn't only exist in my head, this is all I will allow myself.

And if my truth is that I am dying, slowly asphyxiating underneath the ground, then this twisted imagining is infinitely preferable to that dark, cold hell.

So I allow myself to hold onto Luc, to breathe him in, to soak in the feel of being held so tenderly by him. But I don't speak. Don't want to break the spell, to be dragged back *there*, alone and afraid.

I'm jostled, murmured apologies rumbling beneath my cheek as warmth spills over us, and I close my eyes against the wash of the light against my eyes. They only open as he separates us, as I sink into soft material, my fingers gently tugged free from their grip on his shirt.

The noise slips free, then. The pained, almost whimpering noise that sounds nothing like Caterina Corvo. His face appears in front of me, stormy hazel eyes and golden skin smeared with dirt and streaks of red. When his hand curves against my cheek, I turn my face into it, needing that connection to him.

"Little crow," he whispers. "We need to get these ropes off."

This is a beautiful hallucination.

He waits until I jerk my head in agreement, the movement making my neck ache. I bite back the complaint as he steps away from me. Keeping my eyes straight ahead as warm metal slips beneath my bonds, the rasping sound of rope separating into frayed strands, floating away from my skin.

It hurts. Burns, as he takes my hands in his, rubbing them. As he removes my shoes, massaging painful feeling back into my limbs with gentle touches. "Are you hurt anywhere else, little crow? Apart from your face?"

My forehead creases, the tiniest bit of doubt creeping in. Because the pain is increasing as my skin warms up, and with it comes a little more clarity. Awareness, that perhaps this might not be the immediate prequel to the end of my life.

Slowly, I lick my lips. Move them, as if in practice.

But the words are almost soundless. The effort grates against my throat, and I try again. Luc squeezes my hand. "Take your time."

He leans in closer, his ear almost to my mouth.

"Ribs. Sh...oulder."

I think. "S-tomach, maybe."

His hand tightens around mine. "I need to look."

I nod, slowly. "Take this off."

I feel heavy with dirt, as though my body is stained with it. The sudden, desperate urge to be clean washes over me, and I lift my hand, searching for him.

His fingers slide into mine again, and I breathe.

"I want to be clean," I whisper. Words come a little more easily now. "Help me."

My eyes watch Luciano Morelli as he carefully removes my dress. His gaze doesn't linger as his fingers softly probe my body, pressing into spots that make me hiss.

"Two broken ribs," he murmurs. "And your shoulder is sprained. Your abdomen is bruised, here. And your nose is broken. Your cheek needs stitches, little crow."

I blink. I'd almost forgotten about that, about the way Leo's fist smashed into my face, how he dragged the sharp iron edges down my cheek. "Clean first. Please."

But when he carries me into the small bathroom, hazy with steam, I flinch at the sight of the bathtub. At the shape, my body locking up.

"Breathe," he commands gently. "I won't leave you, Cat."

He doesn't. Instead, he climbs right into the tub, holding me to him as he settles into the water, fully clothed. "Look at me," he says firmly when I begin to shake. "Watch me, little crow. You're not there anymore."

He washes me, his strokes firm and gentle as he runs the cloth over my filthy skin while I lean against him. When I reach up to touch my matted hair, he only picks up a jug from the side. Slowly, I relax into him, into the feel of his hands scrubbing my aching scalp. The water around us turns brown with filth, and he empties the water, refilling it twice before he stands.

My arms wrap around his neck, my face buried in his skin as he carries me back out, wrapping a towel around my bare back. My legs cling to his waist, my shoulder and rib burning. Everywhere hurts.

He runs his hand over the back of my head. "I'm going to put you down so I can change. I'll get you something to wear."

I hold myself together, focusing on the pain that flares with every breath as I perch on the bed. He changes in front of me, not bothering with privacy as he yanks on dry sweatpants from the old leather trunk at the bottom of the bed. My arms are guided into a clean, faded white shirt, Luc kneeling in front of me to do the buttons up, threading them through the small holes one by one.

I let him. Let him turn my face towards the light, let him deftly apply the sutures to the cuts in my face, his lips pressed together. Let him give me water, tipping my head back as I swallow small sips that soothe the tightness in my throat.

He tries to persuade me into the bed as he sits beside me, but I shake my head. Instead, I crawl into his lap again, let his arms wrap around me as he shifts backward, settling against the headboard. He pulls blankets up and over us, wrapping them around me until the last of the cold chases from my limbs. His hands stroke through my damp hair. "We should go back," he says softly. "I left my phone – there. Dante was searching too."

A sliver of guilt runs through me. "Tomorrow. Just... not tonight."

I am barely holding myself together here, in this safe, quiet space.

He smooths the hair away from my face, fingers trailing across and down my neck. "Whatever you want, little crow."

***

When I wake, warm and safe and *alive,* curled up in the little double bed in the little white building that now feels like it's ours, Luc is still asleep.

I lie there, watching his face, so close to mine. He looks exhausted, the dirt still there in faded patches on his face. His hands are entangled with mine, still holding onto me.

Keeping me together, as he did last night when I was close to broken. Or maybe I had already broken, and he fixed me. Carefully putting the shattered pieces of me back, like jigsaw pieces slotting into place.

But the morning light shines through the ceiling window, and we don't have the luxury of ignoring the outside world any longer than we already have, in those stolen hours between us.

I carefully pull my fingers from under his. Then I stop, taking in his hands.

The broken, scabbed skin. And his nails – he barely has any left. The damage to his hands, to his strong, sure hands—

My breath catches.

Luciano Morelli saved my life last night. He dug me out of that grave with his bare hands, when I had given up. And he will have the scars to prove it.

I ease my way out of the bed, testing the limits of my body. The pain, I can manage, even though it makes my stomach flip with nausea. It hurts every time I take a breath, a physical reminder of my broken ribs.

But they will heal.

Luc wakes as I'm digging around in the chest at the end of the bed. "Caterina."

I glance up at the rough sound of his voice. His expression is a mix of concern and trepidation. "I have to get back."

The dons are coming today, and I am in no fit state to do battle against my father, or Matteo. But I have to be ready. The consequences of my decisions are waiting for me.

And the fallout, as I return from the dead.

He sits up, the blankets falling away to reveal a swathe of golden skin. "I know. But I wish you'd stay."

Something has changed between us in these hours. Or maybe we gained something back. Something I thought we'd lost a long time ago.

His eyes are on me, almost amber in the light. "Do you ever think about that day?"

My hands clench on the boxers in my hand. "Yes."

I owe him that small truth, after last night.

His smile is sad. "You were the first girl I ever loved, you know. Right from the moment you waltzed up and planted your lips on mine."

My shoulders tighten at the reminder. "I wanted to know what all the fuss was about."

Luciano Morelli. Beautiful, angelic, with those hypnotic eyes and a body that promised sin.

He was the heir all the girls spoke about, in hushed, girlish whispers as they flirted and batted their eyelids at the heirs of the Italian mafia. I didn't understand the attraction.

So when I stumbled across him one day during a Cosa Nostra barbecue, skulking in the grounds of the majestic house we now use for meetings and not much else, I walked up to him and planted my mouth onto his, clumsy and awkward. Then I punched him in the nose out of sheer embarrassment.

He'd staggered back, color springing up on his cheeks as he stared at me and I stared right back. Uncertain. A little lost.

But then he took a step forward and he kissed me back, his arms wrapping around me, warm lips moving over mine.

One day. That's all we had. One single, perfect day. A day of laughter, and fun, and exploring the beginnings of our sexuality in that innocent way that somehow can only happen under the warmth of a summer day.

"The issue," I say quietly, "was that you loved a lot of girls then, Luciano."

I carried him with me when we were apart. Our shared secret, tucked away inside my heart. I could barely wait until I saw him again. The star-crossed lovers of the Cosa Nostra. Romeo and Juliet. And he had promised me that he would wait for me. That we would see each other again.

It all felt so fucking *romantic*, to a dramatic sixteen-year-old Caterina.

Right up until I walked through the doors at the next social and saw him wrapped around someone else. As she smiled at him, soft and pretty and *innocent* in a way that I would never be, and he wrapped his arm around her protectively, tucking her under him as he laughed with the men next to him.

His smile turns sad. "That was a long time ago, Caterina. I was a boy. A stupid boy, with the future of the Morelli family on my head and all the demands that came with it."

And I was a girl. A girl who thought Luciano Morelli loved me, who boasted about it to the others who thought they could capture his attention at the many Cosa Nostra parties we held then.

And how they laughed when they saw how quickly he moved on.

A small moment in my life, considering all that's happened before and since. But one that helped to shape me.

"You taught me that nothing is to be trusted," I say quietly. "Nothing lasts, Luc. Like this – whatever this is. This will not last."

"That's bullshit," he challenges, his brows drawing together. "Judge me if you want to, little crow, but judge me on the actions of the man I am today, not the boy I was seven years ago."

I snatch up the boxers, dragging them up and over my hips, trying not to gasp at the pain. "I'm hardly in a position to judge anyone, Luc. I don't have time for this."

He stands. "So you're running away again."

"I don't run from anything."

I face my fucking problems. Face them and own them.

"Yes, you do. You run from anything that might make that cold damn heart of yours open up," he snarls. "You face danger with a smile, but you run from your feelings like the hounds of hell are chasing you. It doesn't make you weak to *care*, Caterina."

I'm having a lot of feelings right now. Murderous ones. "I do what I have to do to fucking *survive*, Luc. In case you didn't realise, my life isn't exactly fucking daisies."

"So what?" he demands, taking a step closer. "You're going to go through life completely alone? What a sad fucking existence."

I take a breath. "I'm not about to put a target on anyone's back, Luciano. Look at Nicoletta Fusco. Look at *Rosa*. Loving someone in our world will only get them hurt."

He huffs a sarcastic laugh. "Of course they'll get hurt, if you decide to kill them."

The statement makes my chest ache, and his face tightens. In apology, maybe.

But I've had enough.

"I hate you," I snarl. My hands are shaking with the need to run, to fight, to push him away so I don't have to face him. But if I came for a battle, then he came for a war.

"You might hate me," he throws right back at me. "But I have *loved* you since you stole my first kiss and punched me in the nose. So you go right ahead and keep hating me if it makes you feel better, Caterina. Fuck knows I'm used to it by now."

I blink at him as the words sink into my skin, flaying me open. "You... what?"

"Fucking hell, woman," he snaps irritably. "You want it in fucking writing?"

And then his lips smash into mine, his broken hands cupping my battered face.

There is no sign of the gentle Luciano who carried me to bed and cleaned my wounds. This Luciano is the man, not the boy but the heir to a bloody future, and he walks me backward until my aching back presses against the wall. His lips taste both familiar and new, his kiss possessive as his hand slides around to lightly grip my throat.

"I am no victim to be hunted," he murmurs against my lips. "I am a fucking mafia heir, and I am more than strong enough to stand beside you, Caterina Corvo. And you can fight it as much as you want, if you want to waste the fucking energy, but I'm not going anywhere."

He gentles his kiss, brushing my lips up and down, as though he's tasting me, drinking in my scent. "I know what I want. And I'm done waiting, you stubborn woman. So if you insist on going back there today, then I'll be standing at your side."

I swallow, as I let the hope fill me. Tentative, dangerous hope. "You don't know what I've done—,"

"*I don't care*," he whispers. His forehead presses against mine. "Because I know your lines, Cat. I see them, and I am yours anyway. To whatever end."

And I close my eyes. "I...,"

I don't have an answer for him. Not when he's all tangled up in my head, tangled up with Dante and Domenico and the fucking politics wreaking havoc on our lives on top.

"I know. I don't need it, not right now. But I am yours, nonetheless, and I'm so fucking tired of pretending that I am not." He presses his lips against mine once more, and this time I let myself soften for him, pressing back against his heat, our tongues dancing together until the breathlessness is no longer from the aches in my own body but the feeling of his against mine. My hands sliding down his bare chest, hot and aching and wanting.

He pulls away slowly. Reluctantly. "I'll take you back. But try not to die on me. I feel like we've finally made progress today, and it's only taken seven years."

Ass. But my lips still twitch up into a smile.

Caterina

"I'll be fine."

Luc doesn't look at me. Arms crossed, he stares up at my apartment. "Anyone could be in there, Cat."

Truth. But I shake my head anyway, although I at least attempt to meet him halfway. "Wait by here, then. If I let out a petrified scream, you can come dashing to my rescue."

"Hilarious." But he leans against the railing, waiting. There's concern on his face as I move past him, but he doesn't try to stop me again.

As I ascend the steps, I realize that I don't have my keys, but it doesn't matter. The door has been left open, resting against the lock.

And I wonder who waits for me inside.

As I walk in, he doesn't move. Just sits in the leather chair, his head in his hands. For a moment, I think he might be asleep, but then he lifts his head.

"Domenico," I breathe.

He stares at me for long moments. As if I'm a ghost.

He jumps to his feet, moving so swiftly towards me that I don't have time to even lift my hands before his arms wrap around me and he drags me to him, one hand cupping the back of my head as he buries his face in my neck. "Jesus fucking Christ, Cat."

And I melt into him, burying my face into the crook of his neck and breathing him in. "You're here. When did you get out?"

He pulls back with a disbelieving look on his face. "When did I *get out*? When I finally managed to get hold of my fucking men and they told me you were gone, Cat. People nearly died last night and you fucking *disappeared*. Everyone thinks you're dead!"

My mouth opens, and closes again. "Well. I'm not."

I smile weakly, but his eyes are tracing my face, taking in the cuts and the swellings with dawning horror. "It's not as bad as it looks, but watch the ribs. They're broken."

And I watch as the horror turns to anger. His hands are gentle on my skin as he turns my face to look, his finger tracing the sutures. His voice is low when he finally speaks.

"Who did this to you?"

Covering his hands with mine, I pin him with a stare. "Who do you think?"

Ducking away, I cross to the window and wave to Luc. Dom is hot on my heels, and he glowers out through the glass as Luc tips his hand up, his eyes moving between Dom and I before he slowly walks away.

I collapse onto the couch without thinking, and groan, holding my ribs.

That's going to be a bitch to heal.

"Coffee first. Then talk. And can you message Dante to let him know I'm alive? He was looking for me with Luc, but Luc lost his phone in the forest."

When I open my eyes, Dom is staring at me, his arms crossed. "In the forest?"

"Mm." I carefully poke at my ribs, hissing at the pain. Fuck knows what my face looks like. "I might need an ice pack too. I need to try and get this swelling down before the dons arrive. What time is it?"

"Cat." Dom kneels in front of me. "Tell me what happened."

I pause. Try to find the words to explain it. And as the terror starts to rush back in, I slam the door shut, cutting it off. "I... I can't, Dom."

My voice is quiet as I meet his gaze. "Don't ask me. Not right now. I will. But not... not when I need to be as strong as I can be today."

He runs a hand over his face, before he slowly nods. "Not today, then."

When I shake my head, he cups my cheek. "Coffee it is. We have time."

And as he gets up, walking over and pulling open cupboards, the familiar banging ringing it, I savor the feel of having him back. I missed it more than I ever thought I would.

***

Dom shifts to look at me. "Stop that. You'll open your stitches."

"I can't help it," I mutter. We're waiting in the Courtyard, our neutral ground, waiting for the five dons to arrive. And the four heirs, since we're the only ones here.

My finger raises up again and Dom grabs my hand, linking his fingers with mine as he drags it back down to stop me touching it.

"Domenico."

He gives me an unrepentant look when I glance down to our joined hands. "They're not here yet."

I savor the feel of my hand in his for a few more seconds before I pull away. "Any minute."

Luc arrives first, his eyes scanning my face before he comes to stand beside me. Freshly showered, his hair is slicked back on top, his dark blue shirt tucked into his smart black trousers. "Caterina. How are you feeling?"

Dom steps back, but I can feel his eyes boring into the back of my head. "Perfectly well."

I've taken as many painkillers as I can without tipping myself into an overdose, but I'm struggling. Luc flexes his hands, but he snaps his mouth shut as Stefano crosses over to us.

I'm gratified to see his double take, but he stays silent.

I glance around for Dante.

Wondering if Giovanni will show up. And how he might react to seeing me.

It's almost an anticlimax. As the first sleek black car pulls in through the gates, he emerges from the Fusco boundary to my left.

He barely acknowledges me at all, and my gut clenches as he stands next to Stefano. Even Luc glances at him, surprise flitting across his face.

He looks... like an heir. Impeccably dressed, as we all are, in his black shirt and trousers, open at the neck, he stands with his legs slightly apart, his eyes on the cars. His gaze clear.

As if... as if nothing has happened at all.

My mind clouds with confusion, but I purse my lips as Paul Morelli climbs out. Another car pulls in, then another, as Luc heads forward to greet his father. Paul claps him on the shoulder, the murmurs between the two men too soft for the rest of us to hear.

Salvatore Asante is next. I meet his eyes as he gets out, before they drop to the bandage covering his hand. A small smile curves my lips, and I let it happen, let him see it.

I have not forgotten my threat. Nor will I.

His face tightens, fury washing across his expression, but he ignores me as Stefano blocks my view, turning his attention to his son.

Frank V'Arezza is next, his head turning as he frowns. I glance over my shoulder, searching for Dante, but he's still not here. When Frank looks at me in question, I shrug helplessly. "I haven't seen him today."

I glance over my shoulder at Domenico. "Have you heard from him?"

He shakes his head, and concern builds in my chest as a final car pulls through, a solid, silver vintage.

I can't think about him now.

The door opens, and I suck in a breath as Matteo slides out first.

His dark glasses hide his eyes, his blonde hair shaved close to his head as he steps back, clasping his hands in front of him. The picture of a dedicated mafia man.

Cunt.

I can't help flicking my eyes to the side, but Gio gives no impression that he's even noticed Matteo's presence. He just... stands there. And I wonder where Carlo Fusco is.

But my father is getting out, straightening his jacket and striding over to me. "*Carissimo.*"

He kisses me first on one cheek, then the other. But his greeting feels cool, perfunctory. "Greet your cugino, Caterina. Do not be rude."

I'd rather swallow one of my own knives than be cordial to Matteo for a single fucking moment. But I force my head to turn. "Matteo."

He strolls up to me, pulling off his glasses. His lips stretch out, wide and wet, into a grin, teeth gleaming with the platinum caps he had fitted especially, flashing in the morning light. I try not to cringe as his damp mouth meets my cheek, lingering for longer than necessary. "Looking a little battered, *cugina*."

"You should see the other guy," I return swiftly. My father barks out a laugh.

"Excellent. Let us go in, then."

He doesn't mention Dante's absence, but curiosity gets the better of me. "Carlo?"

"He will not be attending."

Gio gives nothing away, his face empty as he turns, following us.

As we walk, my father leans in. "The Fusco girl?"

"Handled." My voice threatens to crack, and I clear my throat.

I sense his surprise as he glances across at me. As if he wasn't expecting my answer. "I see."

We reach the main hall, and I fall into step next to my father, Matteo on his other side. My heels, black today, click loudly on the marble as we walk in.

They acted quickly to clean up the carnage left behind last night. Rows of chairs face the front, all of them filled. This is not a voluntary meeting.

As all faces turn to us, I flick my eyes towards a certain group. Searching.

I don't have to search for long. Leo's face is pale with shock, the men on either side of him staring at me as though I have truly risen from the dead.

I offer them a smile as I sweep past, following my father up to the podium. He sits in the Corvo throne, Matteo and I behind him on each side as the rest take their seats. Gio stands behind his father's empty chair, and murmurs echo through the hall.

A click sounds from behind me, and I turn, pausing.

Dante stands stock still, staring at me. He looks exhausted, still wearing the same suit he had on last night. His shirt is crumpled as hell, scattered with twigs and dirt and who the fuck knows what else.

As if he hasn't stopped searching.

His eyes take in my body, the sharp tailored black suit, the silk red shirt tucked in. The guns at my waist. My daggers, slotted into my shoes and bulking out my sleeves.

My face, battered and bruised.

And he closes his eyes. I see his lips move.

As he strolls past me, his face settling into his usual slight frown, his fingers touch mine. Just barely.

And we face forward.

The five heirs. Matteo. And four dons.

My father stands. He has no need to raise his arms for silence, the room emptying of noise as if someone has flicked off a switch. Someone has set up a microphone on a lectern ahead, and he moves to it.

"What a pleasure it is to be here once again, in the hallowed halls of *mafia university*." His lips twitch as he uses the nickname preferred by many. "To see so many of you here, and to know that the next generation is so focused, is a truly wonderful thing."

He pauses. "But times are not what they once were, my friends. The winds of change are sweeping across our country, making it harder to do the work we once did. All we want is to work as we always have, supporting our communities with transport, protection and more. But the powers that be are finding ever more ways to trip us up."

I've heard this speech. Many times before, in fact. My father uses some iteration of it every time he visits, to *motivate* us.

Most of the time, it has the opposite effect.

But everyone stands straight, paying attention. Nobody wants to catch Joseph Corvo's eye for daring to look *bored*. Or, God forbid, the man standing beside him, a gleam in his eye as he searches the crowd.

"Yes," he says softly into the microphone. "Now, more than ever before, the Cosa Nostra must come together. We must put our petty squabbles aside, and focus on what is truly important. Family. Reputation. *Strength*. Only together may we stand tall against the forces who try to knock us down. Only together, do we rise."

I fight the urge to roll my eyes.

"And in this time of change, protecting the future is of the utmost importance."

My attention sharpens.

"We must prepare for every eventuality, must plan for the unexpected as well as the inevitable. And this, *la mia famiglia*, is the reason for my visit today."

The crowd stirs. I force myself to stay still, keep my face even. As though none of this is a surprise to me.

"In order to plan for the future, one must have a partner to spend it with, no?" My father smiles as my spine locks. "And I am therefore delighted to announce, to you, today, an engagement. *My* engagement."

What the *fuck*?

A smattering of applause breaks out. Matteo leads it, his hands beating together as he glances towards me with a smug smile.

My father holds up his hands with a laugh. "There will be plenty of time to celebrate, my friends. But please, do show your appreciation for my fiancée."

Everyone turns, waiting, as he holds out his hand.

Heels click against the marble noisily as she appears. Her make-up looks heavier, her long, flowing blonde hair curled into a sticky-looking updo as she smiles at my father. As she takes his hand in her white dress, blushing prettily as the crowd breaks into applause.

I do not clap.

I can't.

Because I can't stop staring at Amie – *Amie* – as she leans into my father and he bends to whisper in her ear.

I'm going to be sick.

"Careful, cousin." A murmur sounds in my ear. "You don't seem too happy about this announcement."

As my father turns, his eyes landing on me, I force my hands together, contort my face into an approximation of a smile. "I find myself surprised, Matteo, that is all. Naturally, I'm delighted for them."

My father kisses my best friend's hand, and she laughs, looking for all the world like a blushing bride.

She glances over his shoulder, her eyes meeting mine before she twists to wave at the crowd.

Dismissing me.

***

"That was an unexpected announcement."

I find her out on the terraced balcony, looking out across the Courtyard. We're on the floor above the main hall, in a small room kept exclusively for use by the five dons when they're on campus grounds. Champagne corks pop inside, and I hear a decidedly male cheer as alcohol flows freely amongst the dons and their men.

Amie doesn't turn towards me. She keeps her arms wrapped around herself, her hair barely moving in the breeze as I stride forward, leaning my elbows on the wall that separates us from the ground below. "Not enjoying your engagement party?"

Her lips tighten until they turn pale. "I wasn't allowed to tell anyone."

I push away the hurt. "As though I would have spilled your secrets? I thought we were friends, Amie. He is four decades older than you—,"

"So?" She challenges me. She spins around, her hands clenching. "Not all of us are lucky enough to be born into power, Caterina. Some of us have to take it where we can."

I stare at her, this stranger. Her voice drips with scorn, with loathing, her face twisting into something I don't recognise as she sneers at me. "Is that what you want, then? Power?"

"Better this than to be married off to some lowlife who likes to drink and then use his fists afterwards. At least I will be cared for."

I laugh. From shock, maybe. "You sound like some throwback, Amie. Is this really what you want? To marry him? A young wife to an old man, caring for him in his dotage?"

Not that it would matter, if she truly loves him. But this is clearly not a love match, whatever show my father puts on. He hasn't looked at her once since we've been up here, except to make sure she's behaving.

"This is not the life you want, Amie." I reach out my hand, but she yanks her own away.

"Don't tell me what I want," she says, her voice low. "While you sit there on your golden throne. Are you worried, Cat? That our precious *female* Corvo heir might be displaced?"

I blink. Not at the thought. I'm well aware of the ramifications of this announcement, probably more so than even Amie realizes. But the glee in her words... "When did you start hating me so much?"

She presses her lips together. "When I realized how little you care about any of it. Happy to leave us to our fates while you swan around with your *weapons* and your *men*. You leave at the drop of a hat without a word and come back and expect things to be the same – well I am sorry, Cat. Sorry that I have *changed*, and learned that we have to make our own way in this world wherever we can. I certainly couldn't rely on you, my *best friend*, to help me."

It feels like a slap, her words making me reel.

At the blunt, brutal honesty in them.

And the kernels of truth.

"Fine," I say softly. "I am sorry that I didn't do more, Amie. I wish... wish you had spoken to me. But I wish you the best in your engagement. For a... a long and happy marriage."

Her eyes widen, but I'm already turning away.

I cut through the celebrating crowd, ignoring the stares of Luciano and Dante.

My men.

I glance around as I leave, but there's no sign of Domenico. I ordered him to check on the Crows, to check in on the three injured in last night's smoke attack, and, specifically, to make sure every woman knows to stay inside and keep her doors locked until the dons leave this evening.

I will take no chances with my people when Matteo is around.

The last twenty-four hours are weighing heavily on me, the pain in my ribs radiating out across my body. I need more painkillers, and a chance to clear my head.

So I walk, slowly, back to my apartment. I just need a few minutes without eyes on me.

Dante

Caterina actively avoids my eye as she slips from the room, her hand on her ribs.

My father claps me on the back. "Didn't feel the need to shower for the occasion, then?"

I force a smile. "Apologies again. I lost track of time. Had a little too much excitement at the social last night."

He laughs, thank God, not looking too closely at the tension in my face. "I'm glad to see you relaxing a little more, son."

Glad to think I might have been somewhere other than focused on Caterina, he means.

Making an excuse, I head towards the door.

I have to see her. Just for a minute. Just to hear her voice, to check over the injuries to her face.

I thought she was *dead*.

Searched for hours, through the night and into the morning, ripping apart that forest. Roaring her name until I was hoarse, just in case she was lying injured somewhere. Uncaring that my phone had died until I looked up and realized the lateness of the day.

Bracing myself, as I slipped into the main hall, to see an empty space where she would normally be standing.

But there she was. Standing there, staring at me as if *I* was the lost one, returning home.

My attention is so divided that I nearly trip over the small pile of items on the other side of the Courtyard. Cursing, I catch myself, reaching down to pick up the trash that someone has left here.

Except that it's not trash.

My hands clench on Caterina's daggers, left in a neat little pile. The four that she wears. One in each shoe, one strapped to each arm. When I look down, I see her gun beside the spot where they lay.

Cold invades my body. It's not possible.

Not again.

I run to her apartment, just in case. Praying that I'm wrong.

Nobody answers. When I step back, craning to look through the windows, there's no movement in sight.

But I already knew that would be the case. Because Caterina would never, *ever*, leave her daggers like that.

I slip back into the reception, scanning the room until I meet Luc's eyes. I tip my head, but I keep looking, keep scanning. And then I notice.

He strolls up, leaning against the wall next to me, a brandy in his hand. "What?"

"Cat. She's gone," I breathe.

And so is Giovanni Fusco.

A Murder of Crows Playlist

Find it on Spotify:

Arsonist's Lullaby – Hozier
Start a War – Klergy, Valerie Broussard
Power – Isak Danielson
Missile – Dorothy

On the Rise – Generdyn, BELLSAINT
Game of Survival – Ruelle
Can I – Tedy
Man or a Monster – Sam Tinnesz, Zayde Wolf
Control – Halsey
Battlefield – SVRCINA
How Villains are Made – Madalen Duke
One Last Goodbye – Klergy
Wicked Game – Ursine Vulpine, Annaca
Take Me to Church – MILCK

Stalk Me

If you'd like to keep up with the latest releases, here's how!

Printed in Great Britain
by Amazon